W9-CHD-866

JULIE OLSON—the same hated rival who took away her man is now raising her son—and she is not going to get away with it.

DOUG WILLIAMS—a handsome adventurous con-man, fresh from prison, he comes to town looking for a fast hustle, but instead falls head over heels in love.

ADDIE OLSON—she waltzes back into her daughter's life unannounced, this time to disrupt it in a battle over the same man.

SCOTT BANNING—caught between two women, he'll marry the one he doesn't want, just so he can keep the little boy he's grown to love.

_____

Series Story Editor **Mary Ann Cooper** is America's foremost soap opera expert. She writes the nationally syndicated column *Speaking of Soaps*, is a major contributor to leading soap opera magazines, and is a radio and television personality.

Gilian Gorham, who wrote *Sentimental Longings*, is also a widely published poet. She divides her time between her Manhattan penthouse and her cottage in Beverly Hills.

Dear Friend,

One of the special benefits of reading Soaps & Serials Books is the ability to go back in time and retrace the development of our favorite soap opera characters. Everything we do is based on what has happened to us before. So considering how broken-hearted Alice Horton was about her daughter Marie's love problems in past episodes, is it any wonder that in today's episodes she lends a sympathetic ear to her granddaughter, Hope, as she sorts out her marital problems with Bo Brady?

Book 4 of the DAYS OF OUR LIVES series, *Sentimental Longings,* brings the Horton family to the brink of another crisis. At times like these, Alice's insight is invaluable.

For Soaps & Serials Books,

Mary Ann Cooper

Mary Ann Cooper

P.S. If you missed our previous novelizations of DAYS OF OUR LIVES and can't find them in your local book source, see the order form inserted in the back of this book.

DAYS OF OUR LIVES

4

SENTIMENTAL LONGINGS

PIONEER COMMUNICATIONS NETWORK, INC.

Sentimental Longings

SENTIMENTAL LONGINGS

Chapter One

Escaping the Past

In spite of her vulnerable and ungainly condition, in spite of her nineteen years, Julie Olson sat primly on the edge of her attorney's sofa, in full control of the situation. She was coolly interviewing the parents-to-be of her illegitimate child.

Between broken promises from her parents and the cruel betrayal by her best friend, Susan Hunter Martin, Julie had learned to be wary of mere words. Now, when important decisions had to be made, she had learned to watch and to assess people from behind a mask of queenly graciousness that intimidated many. Those who knew her father, international banking tycoon Ben Olson, recognized her at once. She was now engaged in a decision that could be the most important one in her short lifetime—finding the ideal couple to adopt the child she had to give up.

Scott and Janet Banning sat facing her. Scott's large, raw hand curled protectively around his wife's pale one.

"I grew up on a farm, Miss Olson," he was saying. "We were dirt poor. I never had a toy that wasn't broken or worn-out. . . ."

Julie was looking at Scott, but the real object of her scrutiny was Janet. Her large dark eyes were clear and thoughtful. *Here*, Julie found herself thinking, *is a woman who won't go running in all directions, playing with people, or doing things on a whim.*

". . . and nothing will be too good for that baby," Scott finished.

"I believe you," Julie said quietly. "I know you will be good parents—" She stopped, momentarily overcome, then continued haltingly, "I only want you to promise that no one will ever know—I mean, that no one will ever know the baby was adopted. *You* should be his parents—his *only* parents."

Janet's brimming eyes were filled with compassion. "Of course," she reassured Julie softly and, turning to Scott, said, "You'll promise Julie—and me, too, won't you, darling?"

Scott nodded brusquely.

"Well!" the attorney broke the silence. "Shall we get the papers in order then?"

Once the choice was made and the arrangements carried out, Julie vowed to herself to keep out of the picture. She needed time for emotional healing and the new parents needed time to learn to love their baby.

From time to time over the weeks and months that followed baby Brad's birth, Janet Banning wondered aloud about what Julie would think of the progress little Brad had made. She would never forget the quiet dignity with which the painfully young woman had made her sacrifice, and Brad was such a joy. Scott always replied that the less they thought about Julie, the better. "Let's leave it be, shall we?" he would say. "From here on in, *we* are his parents."

"If it were up to you," Janet said, smiling, "that child would have been born in a cabbage patch, like in those old fairy tales we were brought up on."

"Oh, you think too much, that's all," Scott said. "What is that fancy word they use for it—'introspective'?"

It was precisely that quality that had attracted Julie to Janet Banning. Lately, however, Janet was doing more heavy thinking than usual. What others would call the responsibilities of caring for a baby round the clock, she found to be a joy. Still, she felt a sense of foreboding, a feeling that there was a lot to accomplish before . . .

Hard as she tried, she couldn't finish the thought. Before what? It had to do, in part, with exploring the child's potential. And she would have liked to question Julie as rigorously as Julie had questioned her. Who was the father? What was he like? What traits might he have handed down to little Brad? Janet drew a blank when the pediatrician had asked about Brad's genetic inheritance. All she could say was that the mother was in her late teens, bright, personable, and extremely attractive. Of the father, she knew nothing.

"All we'd have to do would be to write to Martha," she told Scott. Martha was a great-aunt of Julie's, and it was she who had first introduced Julie to the Bannings.

"Leave it alone, willya, honey? Please let's not talk about it right now," Scott replied. "These twelve and fifteen-hour days are going to have to go on for a while, at least as long as the weather's good. After all," he flashed a grin, "we gotta make houses while the sun shines!" When he saw Janet's crestfallen look, he kissed her tenderly. "C'mon, smile—we have all the time in the world, you know!"

But Janet's sense of foreboding continued to hover, like a shadow, around the edges of her consciousness. Either somebody would die before she could find out what she needed to know, or someone would take away their precious baby, or . . .

Again Janet could not complete the sentence. It was all so silly! For the first time in her life she began to have disturbing dreams. She would wake up in the middle of the night and check again on the baby, sometimes only a half-hour after tucking him in. Though she rarely remembered her dreams the next day, or perhaps because of that, she felt haunted and alone.

"Susan again, huh?" Mickey Horton asked

his secretary, Karla. "She sure turns up like a bad penny. Did she say what it was about?"

In the end, he reluctantly agreed to see her.

The new law offices of Mickey Horton, Esquire, were impressively spacious, as was appropriate to his continuing success. Glancing at the understated but undoubtedly expensive decor, the young woman was struck with the thought that she could not possibly afford to have him represent her, or even advise her. Just as she was about to excuse herself, she was ushered into the office of the man who had saved her from life imprisonment—or worse.

"How are you doing, Susan?" Mickey asked, as he gestured for her to be seated. "Staying out of mischief? I assume you are, because I haven't heard a thing." This attempt at light banter was a way of distancing himself from his old client. Mickey had only taken up Susan's murder case as a favor to her mother. Now everything was even. If he ordered her out this minute, he would feel no guilt about it.

Susan silently held out the letter from the bank. While Mickey read it carefully, she nervously twisted and untwisted a frazzled lock of her thick blond hair. When Mickey finished, he looked up and waited for her to speak.

"Is it for real?" Susan asked meekly.

Mickey held it up to the window and let the light shine through the watermark impressed into the expensive vellum paper.

"Looks pretty good to me, as bank stationery goes, that is. Of course I can confirm all of this with a simple phone call or two." He was surprised that his answer did not seem to excite her. Susan had come in looking sadly apprehensive, and so she remained.

Susan Hunter Martin had a great deal to live down and not enough money to do it with. When she shot her handsome young husband to death, the story had made all the papers and even one of the wire services. As one of the reporters had pointed out, she certainly wasn't the first teenage mother who had "blasted her better half." Still, the cartoon of her standing beside the body, holding a smoking, double-barreled shotgun, had stamped her with an image which she couldn't seem to lose.

What made it all so much worse was that she had to hang around a hometown she detested, answering the telephone in a real estate office, while her ex-friend Julie traveled the globe. Florida, Europe, South America . . . Susan too would have traveled, had she the money Julie Olson had. David had never had money, but though Susan would be the first to admit she didn't marry David for wealth, she wouldn't so easily admit that the real attraction had been that he belonged to Julie.

Mickey was now silently scribbling notes to himself regarding other pending matters. After a minute or two, he glanced at his watch as theatrically as he could, hoping to get her to speak up or leave.

"It doesn't matter anyway," Susan said with a resigned shrug. Mickey smiled at the thought of greedy little Susan Hunter about to come into a sizable inheritance and dismissing it. No one, in his experience, could change *that* dramatically in such a short period. Now, for the first time, he wondered if the letter *was* genuine, or if Susan was up to some trick or other.

"Had you ever heard David speak of this Harold Martin?" he asked. "I was under the impression that after David's mother died, he was the end of the line."

He and the baby, Susan thought. Aloud she said, "He mentioned something about his father having a brother who ran away from high school and was never heard of since. I guess that must be him."

"Well," said Mickey, standing up to terminate the discussion, "if none of this matters to you, why bother to consult a lawyer? You didn't need *me* to tell you that the letter *looks* genuine. That much you could have checked out yourself."

"I want to know if I have any say where it should go. I mean, even if I myself will never see a penny of it," Susan said haltingly as she rose to leave.

"Are you planning on renouncing the world and all its riches? Somehow that doesn't sound to me like the Susan I have come to know so well."

"Of course not," she snapped back, with some of her old spirit. "It's just that I know I will never be allowed to inherit anything from David or any of his relatives. That's the law."

Mickey smiled to himself, and gestured for Susan to seat herself again. He leaned back in his chrome-and-leather swivel chair and crossed his well-shod feet on the corner of his desk. "Tell me more," he coaxed. "I like to learn something new every day."

"You're making fun of me!" Susan snapped. "*You're* the lawyer. You know I killed David. You know that nobody can profit from a murder. Otherwise, people would kill their own parents so that they could inherit."

"*Some* people would, perhaps," Mickey said wryly, sizing her up anew, grateful that the two of them were not related. "Tell me, where did you learn all this?"

"I read mysteries," Susan said. "The first suspect is the one who has the most to gain from the will. That's usually the killer, all right."

"Then I'm pleased to let you know that none of that legal reasoning has anything to do with your situation," Mickey said. Susan's expression wavered, as if she could not quite believe what she was hearing. "The characters you read about would presumably be convicted of deliberately, willfully, and in a premeditated manner, murdering someone for gain."

Susan grabbed the edge of her chair as hope began stirring within her. Mickey was making sense. She had done none of those things. She'd merely blown David away. . . .

With a shudder she brought her thoughts back to what Mickey was saying.

"You, my dear, were not even convicted. When someone is acquitted by reason of temporary insanity, he—or she—stands in the same position regarding inheritance as any other good citizen."

Susan had begun to squirm with a rising excitement. "What do I do now?" she interrupted.

Mickey began to detect signs of the old greed and ambition in Susan's gestures. If she were anybody else, he would have an answer ready. But this was the young woman who had nearly ruined the life of his niece Julie. She seemed destined, he thought, to get into trouble and drag others down with her.

"Will you help me?" she asked.

Mickey shook his head. He regarded her as "bad news." "I'm sorry, Susan. I have neither the staff nor the time. My practice is in the corporate law field." He saw her face drop, and added, "It's nothing you can't do yourself, you know. Just take the bus upstate to Woodridge, identify yourself, and the bank will handle it for you. Save yourself a lawyer's fee and come out ahead."

He wanted to add many things, cautions about handling all that money. He wanted to suggest a broker or tell her to invest it in safe bonds or securities. But that might be advice that would come back to haunt him. He shook her hand, wished her luck, and pointed her toward the exit.

A few days later, Susan requested a private meeting with Mr. Knowlton, the head of the real estate office where she worked. He evaded her as long as he could, but her persistence wore him down. "I'm in no position to pay you a raise, and I have all the salespeople I need, and then some," was how he began the discussion.

Susan nodded and brushed aside his comments with disdain. "Don't think of me as a receptionist, or any kind of employee," she said. "Think of me as a client."

Then she proceeded to describe the kind of property she had in mind.

In the end, Susan's ideas were almost what Mickey might have hoped for. She had learned enough about her own nature to hold herself back from impetuous acts. The young girl who had once hocked the family silver for a bus ticket and a few wild days in New York was gradually maturing. She had been sitting beside real estate salesmen long enough to learn the value of a good investment in property; and most of all, she longed for peace and serenity, things she had never known before. Looking through the pictures of attractive country homes, she imagined a simpler life among simpler people, people who would accept her as a neighbor. Somewhere not too far from Salem, but far enough so that she could lose the stigma of that horrible nickname "Shotgun Suzie."

Chapter Two
A Tender Farewell

Susan Hunter Martin first saw the home of her dreams on a cool, overcast morning. The real estate agent begged her to wait until the weather was better, but Susan was eager to get going. "Besides," she pointed out, "I'm not going to be living there only on sunny days."

The rain had eased to a drizzle as they drove off a two-lane blacktop and into a private driveway. "Well, here we are," the agent said as he opened the car door for her. She stepped out onto the circular drive just as the fog began to lift. In front of her stood a house more beautiful than anything she could have imagined. In a vague haze of excitement she noticed a white facade, a deep verandah, and an elegant entranceway supported by graceful white columns. On one side of this wonderful mansion an extended wall of glass overlooked a meadow, at the bottom of which a brook flowed, turning into a waterfall where it tumbled down a steep slope.

"Don't you want to go inside?" the agent asked. Susan shook her head and motioned for him to wait while she explored outside. Mist clinging to her hair like damp diamonds, she wandered through the stillness, pausing by an old-fashioned gazebo tucked away in the back, and luxuriating in the soft sounds of the wind blowing through the trees—maple, crab apple, weeping willow.

Here at last was a haven, a home for both her memories and her future. She thought of how nice it would have been to build a tree house for her baby boy, had he lived. And the garden plot! She and David could have cultivated it, and the baby could have learned how seeds grow into plants. . . .

But the baby was dead and David was dead and life had to go on. She blew her nose and ran a comb through her hair. Now she was ready to explore the interior.

That same day, she signed the papers in the agent's office, paving the way to a real estate closing. Still in shock at this change in her fortunes, she drove back to the house alone. She didn't even get out of the car but, chin in hand, sat looking at the picture it all made. An inner voice said, "But you never took care of a lawn before, and this one is huge!" Then another voice reminded her that she could easily afford a gardener—and anything else she needed.

* * *

Though Janet Banning's headaches and ominous dreams continued, the baby was thriving. Scott reveled in his new son and as often as he could, he took off a half-hour in the middle of the day just to play with him.

"Have you heard about our new neighbor?" he asked Janet one noontime. "I think I caught a glimpse of her turning into her driveway."

"Then she must have been pretty," Janet teased. "You usually keep your eyes straight on the road." She told Scott what she had learned—that the egg man and the dairy man had dropped off notes at their new neighbor's, but hadn't found anyone there. And that the people at the crossroads grocery had said that she probably knew more about her next-door neighbor than they did, except that, from the little she ordered, she seemed to be living alone.

A few weeks after Susan had moved in, she arose one morning with a sense of excitement, and dressed carefully, almost as if she was preparing for a date. She looked around to see that everything was neat, and then laughed aloud to herself. "You'd think I was expecting a group of ladies to tea!" She had no new friends, and wanted no one from her old life to visit her here, spreading rumors that would force her to move. She'd even begged her mother not to give anyone her forwarding address. Convinced that she could never live down her former friend's hatred of her, Susan feared most that Julie

Olson would discover where she lived.

She shook off the bad thought, turned on an easy-listening radio station, and sang along with the music. Today was going to be a lucky day. She felt it in her bones.

Next door, Janet arose with a headache—now they were beginning to last through the night. Taking the matter into his own hands, Scott called their family doctor, and the doctor arranged for Janet to come in that day to take a series of tests. Scott, to reassure her, decided to take the day off to stay with the baby.

Perhaps it was the fog, settling in the valley and touching everything with a soft brushstroke of filmy white, that lent such eerie magic to the scene, to the weeping willow and the old-fashioned gazebo. Susan found herself drawn to the decorative redwood fence which divided her property from her neighbors'. Like a scene out of *Twilight Zone*, there was her dead husband sitting on a swing and holding their little son on his lap. A cry escaped Susan's lips, as if she had seen a ghost!

Of course it wasn't David. As soon as the man approached the fence, with the baby lifted to his shoulder, the wisps of fog could no longer obscure his looks, could not allow her to confuse him with her late husband.

"Hi, there. I wondered when we would finally meet," he said cheerfully. "I'm Scott Banning and this little fellow is Brad."

Take away the fog, the mist, the distance, Susan thought, and little Brad still looked inexplicably familiar. If she hadn't seen her own dear baby placed in his coffin and buried . . . But this was ridiculous! Logic told her that had her child lived, he would have been much older.

All of this ran through Susan's mind in the split second it took to smile and offer her hand over the fence. After she introduced herself, Scott apologized that he and his wife had not welcomed her formally. Then Susan remembered how she had thought, that very day, of entertaining guests.

"Please come over for a few minutes, won't you? I have freshly brewed coffee, and some milk and cookies for little Dav— I mean, Brad. Now that the fog has lifted, we can have our snack in the gazebo. I bet Brad has never even seen one."

When Janet returned that evening, her announcement pushed all thoughts of their new neighbor from Scott's mind.

"The doctor is sending me to a neurologist," she told him in a level voice. "He thinks I may have some problem up here." She pointed at her head.

Scott tried to conceal his alarm. "What can we do?" he said, taking her hand.

"Only wait," she replied. She seemed oddly unconcerned and dismissive, as though it were a minor, inconsequential occurrence. Scott picked up Brad and plopped him in his wife's lap. Then he started tickling, and soon he had them both giggling. But he could see Janet's heart wasn't in it, and suddenly he remembered Susan Martin.

"What's she like?" Janet asked eagerly when he told her he'd met their new neighbor at last.

"Her name is Mrs. Martin, so she is, or was, married. There doesn't seem to be a Mr. Martin in residence."

"You went into a designing divorcee's home alone!" Janet teased.

"No, as a matter of fact. Not only was I chaperoned by my son, but we only got as far as the gazebo."

"Is she lonely, do you think?" said Janet pensively.

"I don't know," Scott answered, touched by Janet's concern for others, even when things weren't going well for herself. Then, brightening, he saw a way for them to take their minds off Janet's impending neurological examination. "Let's have a party," he said. "Just a small one, to introduce Susan to her new neighbors. Who should we invite?"

Nothing worked out the way they had planned, the party never took place. "You'll explain to our neighbor that I'll be out of action for a while?" Janet requested from her hospital bed. Scott nodded as he tried to keep his expression cheerful. Janet had been through a series of brain scans, all of which confirmed the original diagnosis. She had a brain tumor, and it was growing rapidly. A series of radiation treatments was slated, but the results could only delay the progress of the disease, the neurologist had explained.

"The human body can only take a given amount of radiation and survive," he had continued. "We want to delay the treatments and keep them as far apart as we can, to stave off the inevitable."

Janet's way of staving off the inevitable was total denial. Her hospital dresser and bedtable were filled with pictures of baby Brad, and her chatter was filled with longing for him.

One evening, a few days later, Scott called Susan to tell her the party would have to be canceled.

"Oh, I'm sorry," Susan said, noting the catch in Scott's voice. "Is something wrong?"

The sincerity and concern in Susan's voice, and his terrible need to unburden his fears, shattered his usual reserve. He told her everything, how unfair it all seemed, especially since they had waited so long for a baby, and now Janet would probably not live to enjoy him.

"The worst of it," he worried, "is that Janet doesn't seem to accept what's going on. She's a little thing, but she's always been so strong—" His voice broke again.

For the first time in her young life, Susan began to see that hers wasn't the only tragedy. "Maybe it would be a good idea to talk about that with the doctor," she said after a short pause. "I mean, maybe that would help."

* * *

The neurologist referred him to a colleague, Dr. Tom Horton.

"As your neurologist probably told you," Tom said to Scott, "I am basically a family doctor with a fancy title—*internist.*"

Scott nodded. Somehow, he felt at home in the office of this kindly, wise man who had set aside a few minutes in his own busy schedule to comfort a troubled husband.

"She just doesn't listen, Doctor. Whenever any really grim news comes back from a medical test, her eyes glaze over and she talks about our son. This is not the least bit like her. She has never, never been like this before."

"She has probably never been face to face with her own mortality," Tom observed. "None of us knows how we will react until we are abruptly put in that position. And when I say that to you, young man, I'm also thinking about members of my own profession." When Scott looked up surprised, Tom elaborated. "I have seen cancer specialists and heart specialists hold their own X rays and not be able to read them properly."

Scott buried his face in his hands for a moment. Then, in a trembling voice, he asked, "What should I do, Doctor? Should I shout it at her? Should I pretend that everything is going to be fine? Maybe this is the sort of situation where the truth doesn't do anyone any good. . . ."

Tom pulled out a bottle of Scotch that he kept for moments like this, and poured a shot for his visitor. Then he riffled through a copy of Janet Banning's files.

"Well," he sighed. "I see that her doctors have communicated quite properly. In the beginning, you see, we use the word *tumor* and wait a sufficient period of time before introducing the word *cancer*. This usually gives the patient time to adjust to the information. It also allows the doctors to determine how much bad news he or she can take."

He looked up. "Usually," he went on, "it is the family member who cannot deal with the truth. Often the patient protests that she is being kept in the dark, and demands to know everything on the spot. I can see that is not the case with Janet."

"She doesn't want to know. By now that's one thing I'm sure of," Scott said. When Tom didn't respond, he asked, "Are there any reasons for forcing her to accept the truth?"

"Of course not," Tom said. "In some cases, wills must be drawn and updated—"

"Ours is simple. We've left everything to each other. Neither of us would ever think of changing that."

Then the two men discussed a series of practical considerations, and finally Tom backed Scott's conclusion that things should go on in the same way.

"What will the doctors tell her?"

"Whatever she asks them," Tom said. "From what we both know about Janet now, she won't be asking many questions."

At the end of their conversation, Scott again asked, this time with calm resignation, "What can *I* do to help?"

"You must make sure that hope is always held out to her," said Tom gently. "Some of the progress we have been making is most remarkable. Besides, a patient who can believe that there is hope can manage better with less medication and, ultimately, less suffering. If denying is Janet's way of handling it, who are we to criticize?"

As the two men shook hands, Tom said, "I hope Janet realizes what a wonderful and dedicated husband she has."

Scott was well aware that everything would have fallen apart without Susan Martin. During the long periods when Janet was receiving treatment or going through exploratory surgery, Brad found a second home at his "Aunt" Susan's. Scott marveled at the instant and joyful rapport between the two. It helped him concentrate on being there for Janet.

He was especially grateful because he had so little time these days. To stay ahead of the enormous medical payments and other expenses, Scott had to put in many extra hours on construction sites. Then he would rush to the hospital to sit with Janet until visiting hours were over. Dr. Horton had arranged a special pass for the baby to visit his mother one evening a week, but most other times, the child was with Susan, playing in the gazebo, tumbling down the lawn, learning his first words.

Scott remained true to Janet and Susan

respected him for it. Her job was to be a strong shoulder for Scott to lean on. At that moment, if she were asked whom she loved the most in the world, she might have thought of baby Brad.

When Janet's time came, it was a peaceful letting go. She reached for Scott and held his hand and told him to let the baby know how much she loved him. A few hours later, when the pain became too great, she asked for medication, and died in her sleep.

"She really must have known it all along," Scott later said to Susan with an air of astonishment. Impulsively, Susan reached over and hugged him. Up until that moment, the two had hardly touched.

After the funeral, things would change.

Chapter Three
Collision Course

Halfway around the world, another death occurred, one that, for most of the citizens of Salem at least, overshadowed Janet's quiet passing.

Ben Olson's obituary took up most of the back page of the Salem paper and even rated a mention in the *Wall Street Journal*. He was a small-town boy, from a poor family, who had worked his way up to a position of vast responsibility in the world of international finance. He received the same respect in death that he had commanded in life.

Julie regretted that her memory of him was darkened by that last meeting they had had before she flew to Paris. Taking one look at his pregnant, single daughter, Ben had stormed that she was ruining his life and the family name, and then he'd sent her packing. A great deal of her current bitter dissatisfaction could be traced to that fateful meeting. She could still feel that she had lost her father then, not now.

Thinking back, she recalled how much weight he had gained, as if to anchor his growing fame in business circles. That, and the odd ruddiness of his complexion, should have signaled to Julie the possibility of his having high blood pressure and other physical problems. Certainly his frequent outbursts of rage didn't do him any good.

Julie would have flown to Geneva, Switzerland, for the funeral, but her mother said that it wasn't necessary.

"No, dear," Addie said when Julie questioned her again. "The funeral is tomorrow—you can't possibly make it by then."

"You don't mind being alone?" Julie pressed, though she couldn't help recalling the lonely days and nights of her childhood, spent with an endless parade of governesses and baby sitters while her parents tended Ben's business.

"Oh no," Addie said absently, purposely omitting mention of the charming comforts of André, her current ski instructor.

Julie remained in Salem.

Though father and daughter were so much alike, they had never been close. She'd always resented the way he had mapped out her life with the same cold-blooded techniques he'd employed in projecting a millionaire's portfolio of stocks and bonds. She hated the way he'd treated her like a financial asset—a pretty daughter who, with the proper training, and his contacts and guidance, could marry into money and even pick up a title along the way.

Fat chance, Julie thought to herself. At no time had she ever considered such a thing. Life, to her, just happened when you weren't looking. It was almost as if she had gone out of her way to disappoint him. But now she took time out to see where she fit into the current scheme of things.

Within weeks she discovered that she had a sizable inheritance, intelligently invested. As the local banker explained to her, she could live very well on the interest alone without having to dip into the principle, even after she used some of the principle to buy a penthouse in the newest, tallest building in town.

Now what? She asked herself a few days later. She could fly to Chicago or New York to consult with interior decorators, but it just didn't seem to matter. What kept burning in her mind was the remark the building manager had made when he showed her around the apartment. "This would make a perfect nursery," he said. "Even when the child gets older, all you would have to do is . . ."

As his voice droned on, Julie had thought of the perfect baby for the perfect nursery in the most beautiful penthouse in Salem. If she could have foreseen that she would have the money to live in this style, she would have kept her little boy instead of letting Scott and Janet Banning adopt him. So much in life seemed to be a matter of timing, she mused.

There were two people in the world whom she felt she would never forgive. The first was her father, and now he was beyond all hurt or animosity. The second was Susan Martin, who had killed the only man she had ever loved, the father of her baby.

Thinking of the baby she had given up, she clenched her fists in frustration. In the background, the voice of Edith Piaf came over the stereo, singing in French the famous song, "No Regrets." She thought to herself that whoever wrote the words must have been a liar or a fool.

In the first months of her widowhood, Addie Olson regretted that André, her charming young ski instructor, had emigrated to Quebec so soon after Ben's death, for he would have been perfect to help her through the transition. Those last years in Geneva had taken a lot out of her, when Ben had put on an enormous amount of weight and his blood pressure had shot up, along with his legendary temper. In self-defense, Addie had spent more and more time on the ski slopes with André, and the fact that he could speak to her easily in English helped considerably, for neither of the Olsons could speak any language but their own. As it turned out, Ben had had an interpreter and Addie had had André. . . .

Now she had substantial wealth at her disposal, and no one around to spend it on.

She moved on to Vienna, where she ate her heart out over the most exquisite fancy foods and pastries in the world. Seated in a sunny cafe and spooning dollops of whipped cream—which the Viennese called *schlag*—into her coffee, she would watch the trays of pastries roll by, picking one of this and one of that until she had put on twenty unnecessary pounds.

One day, after examining herself in her full-length hotel room mirror, she called the desk and arranged to check out, deciding to flee the country that had been so generous to her waistline.

In Naples, a few extra pounds of flesh on an attractive and wealthy woman was quite acceptable, even desirable. Addie, though, was more concerned with the weight problem of her luggage, and the few extra items which would invite customs inspection.

The inspector found his wink and smile returned by the wealthy American woman, and he passed her through with a friendly pat and a pinch. He was ready to drop the rules any time if it could lead to a bit of fun. He took Addie to Mount Vesuvius and on a side trip to Capri. One does not diet in the land that is home to fettucini and tortellini and cannelloni. She tried her best to refuse the Italian pastries, but Mario teased her into trying his, and then ordered more. Later, he would slip into the hotel with her, and in the privacy of her bedroom they would share other pleasures.

"I cannot see you for a while, Signora," Mario announced out of the blue one day. He had just emerged from the shower, and was still toweling his tanned, handsome body.

Addie looked startled. As she waited for the rest of his statement, she marveled at how well he had learned English. Of course, she admitted to herself, he really had no choice. At this stage in her life she was not about to start learning "all those foreign languages." She looked at him questioningly.

"It is my wife," he said, sitting beside her on the bed and taking her hand. "She is about to have our seventh child and I feel it is my duty . . ."

She didn't have to hear the rest. It should have been up to her to ask him if he had a family. She thought that by not asking, she would never have to know. No such luck!

There were stone fences and tall elms and winding roads that invited long, pensive walks. By now, Susan and Scott strolled hand in hand, she telling him about her past—the tragedies and mistakes—in an effort to take his mind off his own. She told him simple things, too, things that Janet would have found out the first time she played hostess, but that first time had never come.

The fact that Susan was widowed rather than divorced or separated came as a surprise to Scott. The further information that she had lost her baby boy in his infancy came as less of one. There was something about the love and support that she showed toward little Brad that suggested her experience as a mother.

And so, by the time the rest of her past had come pouring out, the two of them knew each other's sorrows so well that Scott accepted everything in the kindest possible way. When walks gave way to long bike trips, each of them had a baby-seat attached to the back of the bike so that they could take turns toting little Brad.

Susan helped Scott to find a daily house-keeper, but would allow nobody else to take care of the baby. During the days when Scott was at work, Brad played with Susan at her house. She bought a miniature shovel, rake, and hoe so that he could "help" her plant and care for her small garden. On rainy days she would read to him from an ever-growing pile of children's books. If a stranger had had a look at Brad's toys, books, and records divided between the two houses, he would have been hard put to guess where the child actually resided.

Susan had read that the first year after the death of a spouse is harder on a man than on a woman. Evidently, a man alone thinks less about taking care of himself, eating sensibly, getting enough rest. Scott brought out a tenderness in Susan that would have surprised her own mother. She didn't have to be told how grateful he was. It was apparent in his eyes, his gestures, his words, and his gifts. Beyond gratitude lay an area she didn't want to think about.

And beyond gratitude was an area that Scott was warned not to think about. "Take it easy," his close friends told him. "Now is the time when you are just too vulnerable. You owe it to the memory of Janet and the future of your son to go slowly and not commit yourself to this woman or any woman for at least a year. Later, when you get your bearings, you'll be able to think more clearly."

Scott's friends and neighbors did not neglect the new widower, and he received many invitations for parties and dinners. An extra man is a welcome addition to any dinner party, and there seemed to be barely enough men to go around before they all got grabbed up, as one hostess complained to another.

It was just the opposite for the newly single woman. What with suburbia overflowing with recent divorcees and even a widow or two, hostesses felt as if they were taking their lives in their hands if they invited any of them. The feeling was that every unattached woman was on the prowl for somebody's husband—*anybody's* husband. Scott got more invitations than any one person could handle. Susan received none.

She encouraged him to go. She thought that if anything was to come of their relationship, it would have to endure such tests. Scott had loved only Janet since high school and had known no other woman as a friend until he met Susan. There was something else on her mind, though, which she barely admitted even to herself: a constant resentment that she was never anybody's first choice. The father she had adored had discarded her along with her mother when he obtained a divorce. The husband she had tricked into marriage went to his death in love with Julie Olson.

So Scott, more to humor Susan than for any desire to sample his neighbors' cooking, began making the round of dinner parties. The more he went out, however, the closer was the reunion with Susan. Gradually, tentatively, they began to explore the possibility that they were falling in love. It seemed, in a way, too good to be true, and both were careful to do nothing that might extinguish the flame before it had properly started to burn.

Susan once told him jokingly that she loved him because he reminded her of his son. But for the life of her, she couldn't see any resemblance. Perhaps the baby took after Janet's side of the family, she reasoned.

Though they had discussed everything else freely, Scott had stubbornly stuck to the oath made with Janet and the baby's mother, and had never told Susan that Brad was adopted. He hadn't ever lied about it. He just allowed Susan to assume that Brad was their natural child.

Handsome and financially secure, if a bit dull, Scott was as popular an escort for the suburb's eligible women as he was a guest for the hostesses. But after leaving several young women on their doorsteps with nothing more than a smile and a handshake, the gossip started to circulate.

"That's ridiculous," one of the other women said, "of course he likes women. He and Janet had one of the happiest marriages I've ever seen."

"It's probably that neighbor of his who's taking up all of his time and energy. Put a widow on one side of a fence and a widower on the other, and—watch out! Varoom!"

They all wanted to know who the widow was. "*What* Mrs. Martin? What's her first name?" asked one. After digesting the scraps of not very accurate data, the neighbor mused, "Well, if she comes from anywhere around Salem, I can always ask Julie Olson. If she's anyone worth knowing, Julie will have the lowdown on her."

Bill Horton met Doug Williams while they were both assigned to a stint in the penitentiary laundry. Bill generally didn't let it be known that he was a doctor, because anyone who knew anything about chemistry was constantly consulted on how to brew homemade alcohol or concoct some sort of illegal drug. "The less anyone knows about you, the better," an old timer had told him on his first day, and it had been good advice.

Doug, who had gone through several aliases as well as through several bank accounts, laughingly called himself a mathematician. Anything to do with numbers interested him—juggling them, changing them to his advantage, making book on them, or creating innovative financial scams designed to lure the unwary.

Their intelligence and variety of interests set the two men apart from most of the other prisoners, and they became fast friends. One day, Doug pointed to a pin-up over their worktable and asked Bill, "Could you go for that one?"

Bill looked up. Someone had stuck on the wall a poster depicting Susan Martin blasting away with a shotgun. "I didn't before she was famous, and I certainly wouldn't now," he said, before he could stop himself.

Here was something to talk about! Doug seized on the story. "You mean to tell me you know a genuine celebrity?"

After a promise from Doug not to repeat any of it, Bill told what he knew. "Actually, she was a high school kid when I knew her, the best friend of my niece."

"She got off on temporary insanity, then?" Doug asked after Bill had related some of the story. Before Bill could answer, Doug started a long speech on the "abuses" of psychiatric testimony. "Those guys lend their prestige and powers of persuasion to really lay it on the jury. Shrinks are nothing more than flimflam men. I wouldn't trust the best of them. If you've got the money to pay them, they'll lie through their teeth for you. If you don't, you can rot in jail or get the chair."

Bill continued folding the laundry, not trusting himself to answer. The "shrink" who had helped get Susan off was the woman he loved, Laura. She had since married his own brother, and that was partly why he was here. But the stream of thoughts triggered by this recollection was disturbed by a direct question from Doug. He pointed to the picture and asked Bill, "She was rich, right? She was probably able to get the best witnesses money could buy."

Bill shook his head. "There was only one psychiatrist," he said quietly, "a woman she had been seeing for emotional problems before any of that happened. The psychiatrist didn't get paid. She believed, as I believe, that Susan heard that her beloved child was killed and that her husband was responsible. The gun happened to be at hand when her husband told her, and she just went crazy. If she'd had time to cool off and think about it, probably nothing would have happened."

"She lost her kid, huh?" Doug asked. "Yeah, yeah, that's hard—a young mother . . ." A brief look of understanding and compassion flitted across his face, and then disappeared, replaced by thoughts of money. "But you didn't answer my question. Was she rich?"

"Not *then*," Bill responded absently, "although I hear that she's come into some money since. She's gone and bought herself a big house somewhere out of town and seems to be, as my mother would put it, 'quite comfortable.'"

Doug busied himself with folding and sorting the laundry. He and Bill had previously tossed ideas around regarding what Doug should do, since he was due to be released a few months earlier than Bill. He now wanted to learn all he could about Salem and its environs: romancing Shotgun Suzie would be his next "project." As long as there were no firearms around, he should be relatively safe, according to what Bill had said. And if he played his cards right, he might turn out to be relatively rich as well.

Julie's first thought was that Susan Martin, the woman who had once been her best friend, would have to die. But Julie's rage, unlike Susan's, which worked on a hair trigger, seethed until she got it under control.

In this respect, Julie was her father's daughter. "Get all the information you can about whatever is troubling you," he had once instructed her when she was still in high school. "Remember, knowledge is power. Once you know more than those around you, you can get whatever you want. And you can grab it before they know what's hit them."

It wasn't the usual sort of advice a father gives his daughter, but then Ben had been neither a typical father, nor a typical businessman.

"For me," he would say, "money's the goal, and the key to money is information!" By "information," he meant not only the publicized statistics on stocks, bonds, and the health of major industries and industrialists around the world. "Information" was also the backroom whispers, the vengeful slanders, even facts bought and paid for with unimaginable sums.

Wherever there was a crack in the wall, a weakness that others could barely discern, Ben Olson went in for the kill. The first even his colleagues might know that one of Ben's companies had gobbled up a competitor and attached the two names with a hyphen, would be the notice in the *Wall Street Journal*.

But for Julie, money was merely a commodity, which sometimes stood in the way of what she wanted. Throughout her childhood, money had stood in the way of parental love. Ben and Addie spent most of their time wining and dining business acquaintances or traveling to distant places in search of bigger deals and better contacts. Ben, at least, never knew how much Julie envied classmates from homes with much lower incomes where love and emotional support were available twenty-four hours a day. As it was, her attitude toward money and prestige only irritated and sometimes enraged her father.

Susan's parents were first separated, and later divorced, which left Mrs. Hunter on the prowl for a successor to Mr. Hunter. Late evenings at the club and long weekends or weeks following the sun to the "right" resorts where eligible males were rumored to frolic separated her from her daughter, just when the girl needed her most.

Julie and Susan, both lonely and with too much time on their hands, soon occupied themselves by getting into mischief. They were soon collaborating on shoplifting and other misdeeds, a bond that was broken when Susan tricked David Martin into marriage and then refused to divorce him, as promised, once their baby was born.

Julie was incensed when she discovered that, after killing David, Susan had continued to call herself Mrs. Martin. Now, rumors reached Julie that Susan was moving in, however innocently, on her only living tie to David. The nosy neighbor had indeed asked Julie what she knew about this Susan Martin one afternoon when they ran into each other at the supermarket.

"Why do you want to know?" Julie asked cagily.

"Well, she seems to be occupying a lot of Scott Banning's attention these days—oh! I have to run! There's Joan now—"

In her haste, she neglected to mention that Scott Banning was now a widower. So Julie put some of Ben Olson's money to work by hiring a detective.

This was one of the easiest assignments Buck Harris had ever handled. When the stunning young woman entered his tired old office in the Newspaper Building and stated her request, he would have been delighted to grant it to her for next to nothing. He didn't have to catch someone in bed with someone else's spouse. He didn't have to tap a wire, peek through a keyhole, or do any of the other chores that used to make him hate himself in the morning.

When Julie refused a cigarette and waved him ahead with his cigar, he made much of clipping the end off the cigar, sniffing it, and lighting up, to see if his new client would reveal anything of herself by nervous gestures or signs of impatience.

Julie sat up straight in a chair designed for someone to sink into. As usual, she was poised and alert, with hands folded across her purse and a smile glued in place, forcing Buck to break the silence.

"Is there anything of an illegal nature going on here? Anything dangerous?"

She waved his questions aside. "It's exactly what I told you. I merely want information obtained in such a way that no one knows that an inquiry is being made. If that's too complicated for you to understand . . ." She let the sentence dangle as she gathered up her things to leave. It was a technique she had seen her father use to great effect when someone was sitting on the fence, and she was happy to see how fast it worked for her now.

"Take it easy, little lady," Buck protested, with gestures of enthusiasm which almost cost him his cigar. He grabbed it from the desk where it had fallen, popped it back in his mouth, and quickly reviewed the notes he had just taken.

It was indeed simple. He could be a census taker, a pollster, almost anything. He merely had to ascertain the state of two households. The first was the residence of Scott and Janet Banning and their little son.

Then he had to check on Susan.

"You wanna know if this Susan is playing around with Mr. Banning?"

"That's only part of it," Julie replied. "I want to know if she has become friendly with the baby. Has she offered to babysit? Has she invited the child over to her place? Where does she fit in and where does Mrs. Banning fit in? It looked to me like—" Julie stopped, unwilling to reveal what she herself thought. Then she rephrased. "People were under the impression that the Bannings were a very happy couple. Has this woman Susan come in and broken up their marriage?"

By the time Julie left Buck's office, he stared at the retainer she had left and shrugged his shoulders. The check itself was generous enough and the job sounded easy. But the young woman was truly an ice maiden. She wouldn't crack a smile or relax for a second. Nevertheless, if he satisfied her exacting requirements, maybe he could get a little more business from the classy side of town she represented.

As hard as he thought, he couldn't quite figure out Julie's role in the entire scenario. Who was she most interested in? The wronged wife? The guy who was playing around? The mysterious other woman named Susan?

The possibility that the baby figured into the equation never occurred to him. His work as a private eye dealt mainly with triangles. Either that, or tracing deadbeats who ran out on their overdue payments.

The final thing he had to find out was whether this Susan had rented her place or bought it. If she had done the latter, where did she get the money?

Within a matter of days, Buck was able to find out all the important points. When he called Julie he gave her a choice of coming to his office or waiting for a written report. Julie came down the very same day. She glanced at the funeral announcement concerning Janet Banning and a photocopy of the hospital report regarding her inoperable tumor. Then came the photostat of the deed to a house which had been purchased in cash by Susan Hunter Martin.

"If you had only told me it was Shotgun Suzie, I could have found the rest out easier," Buck said, as he handed her the details of Susan's inheritance via David Martin's family.

Finally, Buck was able to confirm that Scott Banning and Susan were an "item." Scott was no longer considered an eligible widower but a man in love, and perhaps on the verge of marriage.

"The baby?" Julie prompted, leaning forward with such tension that the veins stood out in her neck. "What about the baby?"

Buck looked at Julie with amazement. The young lady's intensity was the first sign she'd shown that she was truly human. "Yeah, just a minute," he said, "I was getting to that."

He told her that by now the baby practically regarded Susan as his mother, and that when Scott was at work the baby stayed with her.

When Julie stood up to leave, it was with clenched fists. No betrayed husband, battered wife, or other put-upon client had ever looked as single-mindedly enraged as did this one, younger and more attractive than any of them. Buck didn't know whether to feel more sorry for Scott Banning or Shotgun Suzie Martin. Something was going on and he was glad that his role in it was drawing to a close.

"One final thing," Julie added. "I'm going to want a complete report of all this in writing. And my lawyers are going to want you to make yourself available if and when it becomes necessary. You will be well paid for whatever additional time is required of you."

"Just one question, lady," Buck smiled. "I don't mean to pry, but prying *is* my business, you know." Julie looked back at him impatiently. "You don't have to tell me, but what do you need my reports and testimony for?"

"A child-custody battle. I'm arming myself with the best lawyers, and anyone else I need—which may include you."

As Julie's stiletto heels clicked down the stairs, Buck thought to himself that any lawsuit with Julie at the helm could be the battle of the century.

Chapter Four
A Trial and a Verdict

Until Julie came into her inheritance, her Uncle Mickey was the only lawyer she really knew. Right now, he was the last lawyer she wanted to consult. Aside from a possible conflict of interest, she was also afraid that he might try to talk her out of instituting the lawsuit. She did not want any members of the family advising her on what to do "for your own good, dear." She wanted a lawyer-for-hire to do as satisfactory a job as a detective-for-hire had just done, someone who would know her rights in the matter, and who, if the time came, would fight as hard and as dirty as she was willing to pay for.

Once again she traded on her father's name and money. A quick call to his New York lawyers put her in touch with a local firm that would cooperate completely. "They'd better," she was promised. "We send them all the business we have out your way." She promised, at their request, to report back on their performance.

Now, seated in Rupert Marks' office, she laid out all the reports Buck Harris had prepared for her, together with the relevant adoption papers.

"What's this about a possible conflict of interest between you and Mickey Horton?" Marks asked.

"He defended Susan in her murder trial and got her off," Julie responded. "I never completely forgave him for that. He wasn't even paid to do it. He agreed because he was a friend of Susan's mother." As Marks scribbled notes on a long yellow legal pad, another thought came to Julie. "Besides, the woman who is now his wife is the psychiatrist whose testimony got Susan off."

"Really?" asked Marks, with a sudden renewal of interest. "On what grounds?"

"Temporary insanity." Julie sensed that she now had this debonair and unflappable attorney's complete attention. She related how Susan had been directed to Dr. Laura Spencer months before the killing because of her supposed emotional problems.

"What do you mean by 'supposed'?" Marks asked, arrested by her bitter emphasis on the word.

Julie, unable to hold herself back any longer, spewed out her hatred. "The trial was totally unfair!" she cried. "She killed the man I loved, the father of my child. She should be spending the rest of her life in jail, and after that, burning in hell!"

Marks calmed her down and rang for coffee. Then he went to the sideboard and pulled out a cut-crystal decanter. "It's my specialty, you know," he offered smoothly. "Irish coffee." Julie took several sips and pulled herself together.

"Feel better now?" he asked her. When she nodded, he continued, "Then let me be perfectly straight with you. You may not like what I'm going to say, but you are paying me well to advise you. My message is—you want to have it both ways, and you can't."

"What do you mean?" Julie demanded.

"It is in your interest that Mrs. Martin received a just and fair verdict. You don't realize how much it is to your advantage that your uncle got her acquitted on the grounds of temporary insanity. It's even better that a psychiatrist was able to lay the groundwork for the verdict by showing a long history of emotional troubles."

Marks buzzed again for his secretary. When she appeared with her shorthand book and pencil, he said, "I want a copy of the entire court transcript of *The State* v. *Susan Martin*. Here are the relevant dates. Then I want a special section prepared by one of the clerks dealing with all of the psychiatric testimony. Duplicate it, highlight all the salient points." He thought for a moment as the secretary made notes, then went on, "I also want a complete list of all of Dr. Laura Spencer's credentials."

He dismissed her with a nod and turned to

Julie. "The point we will make to the court, should it become necessary," he said, "is that you handed over your child with the understanding that he was to be raised in a stable household comprised of one Janet Banning and one Scott Banning, happily married for a number of years and hand-picked by you as the perfect couple to adopt your child."

Julie's eyes brimmed over as she remembered. "Especially Janet," she said. "Oh, Scott seemed pleasant enough, but she was so decent and level-headed and sympathetic. *She* was the key to my decision."

Marks got up and paced the room, looking at her approvingly. "Good, very good. I'll want you to phrase it exactly that way if we have to go to court."

"What do you mean by 'if'?" Julie demanded. "Isn't that why I hired you?"

"Yes and no," he responded. "It is always in a client's favor if one can negotiate privately. It's simpler and vastly less expensive. Court is often the last resort."

"You still haven't explained what you mean about my wanting to have it both ways," Julie said. "I think I understand, but I wish you'd spell it out."

"It's quite simple, Miss Olson. We're going to try to show that Mrs. Martin is absolutely stark, raving bonkers. That she's run off the rails, lost her reason, is a candidate for a funny farm. The same testimony that exonerated her the first time is going to catch up with her this time. Once we parade our witnesses and show our testimony, no judge would dare let a child be placed within a mile of the woman."

A small, tight smile of satisfaction crept over Julie's face.

Susan Martin looked at the man she loved in astonishment. "But Scott, darling, why were you so hush-hush about the fact that Brad was adopted? It doesn't matter one bit to me now that I know. I love both of you just as much. What was the big secret?" Even as she spoke, Susan realized that Brad would have *had* to be adopted. As the months went by, he seemed less and less like either of the Bannings.

When Scott explained sheepishly to Susan that it started as a promise to Janet, Susan did her best to downplay it, and assured him it didn't matter in the least. But nothing she said could make a dent in his look of sheer desolation.

"Please tell me what's wrong. It's not Brad, is it? He was fine when I kissed him earlier and read him his good-night story."

Scott turned around and wiped his eyes with his sleeve. Then in a heavy voice he said, "His mother wants him back."

"Wants Brad back? She can't do that, can she? He was legally adopted, wasn't he?"

"Yes, but Julie says . . ."

"Julie!" Susan almost screamed the name. Then she pulled herself together and said, "Julie who?"

• • •

The case finally reached Domestic Relations Court, just before the adoption was due to become final. On the first morning, Julie shot a look of such pure hatred, powerful as a laser beam, amplifying and then focusing with a frightening intensity, that Marks, who had earlier warned Julie to show no emotion, tried to get between her and the judge, to block her expression.

In that one look, Susan saw her prospects for peace and serenity and happiness crumble. She had so much more to lose than Julie Olson! *It's not fair!* she almost cried out, barely able to restrain herself. *This is my life! Not Julie Olson's!*

It was a defeated Scott Banning and Susan Martin who were instructed to prepare the child for his transfer back to his natural mother. As a single father, Scott would be unacceptable as a parent who must provide for the emotional welfare and nurturing of such a small child. When Mrs. Martin was added to the picture, the combination was out of the question.

Laura's compliance with the summons to testify had been reluctant. She had even phoned Julie and asked if the entire process couldn't be managed in a kinder way. Julie's answer was, "I'll do whatever it takes. It will take whatever my lawyers tell me to do."

Although Laura was still concerned about Susan's emotional welfare, there was no way that she could take back what she had said earlier.

As for Julie, the look of helpless dejection on Susan's face was worth almost everything. She shook Marks' hand and added a bonus to the check, then made an appointment with a professional department-store shopper who was to assemble furnishings for a little boy's room and an assortment of clothing, from which Julie intended to select the very best.

"The baby's name, madam?" she was asked.

"David," she answered.

After that it just wasn't the same between Scott and Susan. Perhaps it was because the baby who'd brought them together was being taken from them. Perhaps it was just an overriding and pervasive sense of defeat. Perhaps it was that every other thought was about Brad.

"What do you mean, she sent everything back?" Susan asked, almost in tears. "Those are all his clothes, his favorite toys. Brad can't go to sleep without his little teddy bear."

She looked around the room at the cartons, still neatly packed. Julie hadn't even bothered to open them. "Poor Brad," Susan sighed.

"You mean, poor David." In answer to her startled look, Scott explained that Julie had officially renamed him David.

There was very little to say after that. Each of them went through a private period of mourning. Scott, who had never sought comfort in alcohol, threw himself more and more into his work. He stayed at the construction site until well after dark and then went drinking with anyone on the crew who cared to join him. Food was a matter of indifference to him. He grew thin and drawn and spent much of the night awake, longing to see the little boy he still thought of as his son.

Susan's thoughts went round in circles. Now she knew what had attracted her to the little boy in the first place: He was David's child and looked it. *I made one major mistake in my life that turned out to be a beaut,* she said ruefully to herself. From that moment she'd seduced David, everything in her life had started going downhill. She began to wonder if indeed there was any sense at all in going on. Only one thing was she sure of: she still loved Scott, and she was pretty sure that Scott still loved her. That alone was reason enough to keep on going. That night, she went to sleep all alone except for the little boy's favorite teddy bear.

Within weeks they began seeing each other again, but still, things just weren't the same. Although Scott replied to her questions with vows of love, he seemed strangely distant, as if his mind was miles away.

It was a hard-fought, hard-won battle, and at first the winning itself was a great turn-on for Julie. By the time the baby was delivered to her, the condominium penthouse had gone through a complete transformation. The nursery door said "David's Room," and many of the toys also bore his name, as did his baby cup and bowl. When he was able to read and write, that would be the first name he would know; from the moment he arrived that was the name by which he was addressed.

Concerned about the effects of the trial on Susan, Laura Spencer was especially concerned about the effects on the baby, and begged Julie to reconsider. Julie, however, still resentful of her aunt, refused to listen. Laura found a sympathetic listener in Julie's grandmother, Alice Horton, who volunteered to approach Julie herself.

"For a child that age first to lose the woman he considered his mother, then to lose his father and the woman who was gradually replacing his mother to the courts, is almost too much in itself. But to lose his own name in the process—that could be traumatic."

"I don't see anything wrong with carrying on his father's name. David was a father any child would be proud of," Julie replied.

"Maybe some day, when he's old enough. But now, it could be . . ." Alice hesitated, as if trying to capture the right word or phrase, "emotionally stunting."

Julie stood up as her face colored with rage. Alice was taken aback, and then recalled the look she had seen so many times on Ben Olson: the blazing eyes, the red blotches, the throbbing temples. It looked equally unbecoming on Julie. "Grandma! You don't sound anything like yourself. You sound like your daughter-in-law, the psychiatrist!"

"Why, whatever do you mean?" asked Alice, who knew exactly what Julie was talking about.

"Either that, or you're taking an intensive course in psychiatry yourself," Julie snapped. "I've never before heard you speak of anything being 'emotionally stunting' or 'traumatic.' Never ever! And just a few minutes ago you talked about the 'process of emotional bonding' between mother and child." Julie paced back and forth angrily. "Has Laura been writing your scripts?"

Ignoring her granddaughter's taunts, Alice pleaded, "Why won't you at least speak with Laura? I'm sure that she has the baby's best interests in mind—"

"Because my Aunt Laura's 'expert' testimony got Susan off a murder charge and set her scot-free!" Julie shrilled. "And my Uncle Mickey ran the whole show as lawyer for the defense. Those are two family members I don't care to trust for advice regarding *my* welfare or my *son's* welfare, thank you!" The highly charged atmosphere told Alice that Julie had been bottling up her feelings for a long time. In a low and seething voice, Julie went on, "I'd hate to feel that I couldn't trust *anyone* in the entire family, Grandma."

So many thoughts ran though Alice's mind. She could point out that both Mickey and Laura were only doing their jobs; that they were both people of great integrity who would never compromise professional ethics or personal beliefs, regardless of the situation. She said none of this.

Knowing generations of Hortons, children and grandchildren, had given Alice Horton a sense of perspective and a sense of when to speak out and when to keep silent. Julie was so overwrought that one wrong word might sever her relationship with her troubled grandchild. In that process, she might have cut herself off from her first great-grandchild. *Brad or David,* she thought to herself, *whatever she calls him, it will work out in the long run as long as the family sticks together.*

Alice rose, placed the present she had brought on the coffee table, and kissed Julie on the cheek. "I had no idea how late it was," she said, taking her leave. "Give me a call when you can let me know how . . ."—here she hesitated almost imperceptibly before going on—"how *David* likes the toy I brought him."

Julie returned the kiss as if nothing had happened, but her triumphant expression said, *See, it wasn't so hard to say* David, *was it?* The child was napping and the women had been passing the time until he awakened. But now they both came to the conclusion that it was time for taking leave. Each breathed a sigh of relief that nothing was said that needed unsaying. Their relationship would endure.

Chapter Five
A Proposal

Laura Spencer held the envelope in her hand as gingerly as if it were burning. Inside was information on a matter dealing with a man she had gone out of her way to forget, an old flame, if the term were not too hopelessly old-fashioned; a man about whom the only good thing she could say, if pressed, was that through him she had met her husband. And even that was not deliberate. The name inside the envelope was Bill Horton.

Laura noted with surprise that the hand holding the envelope was trembling. She put it down on her desk and put her head in her hands as all the memories came flooding back. How did that old quotation go? "Physician, heal thyself"? Laura was not only a physician, but a psychiatrist. She had a top position at Salem General Hospital, a waiting list of would-be patients, and a thriving practice. In addition, she had to her credit dozens of important psychiatric papers printed in such prestigious medical journals as the *Journal of the American Medical Association* and the *New England Journal of Medicine*, as well as in several psychiatric journals.

Because of her credentials, Laura was often called out of state as an expert witness at important trials. One had involved an attempted assassination, others had involved murder, and most had achieved wide newspaper coverage in which her name was prominently mentioned.

It was with this in mind that the board of directors and administrators of Salem General Hospital selected Laura to investigate the case of Head Surgeon William Horton. At the time she'd pleaded that she was already overloaded with cases and had committed herself to some new out-of-town court assignments.

"That's precisely why we've chosen you," she was told by one of the administrators. "A psychiatrist with your credentials will be listened to. Your judgment will be more easily accepted by the community at large as well as the board of directors."

The administrator seemed unaware of the fact that Laura, who practiced under her professional name of Spencer, was actually Laura Horton, Bill's sister-in-law. Since that would have no bearing on the case, Laura never mentioned it, but what she never would have revealed, under any circumstances, was the fact that Bill had raped her.

Now everything was coming back to haunt her.

Long before that horrible day, she and Bill had dated when they were interning at the Upstate Medical Center, and had even become engaged. When Bill became traumatized because a nerve impairment in his right hand prevented him from continuing a brilliant surgical career, he'd run away from Laura and everyone else.

To escape from her memories of desertion and what she concluded was a broken engagement, Laura came downstate to Salem General Hospital. It was here in Salem, where she was called in to testify on behalf of one of Mickey's clients, that she'd first met the charming and brilliant attorney who became her husband.

That was what Bill couldn't take. He apparently expected everything and everyone he'd left behind to remain in place awaiting his return. After almost a year of silence, he came back to find the love of his life married to his brother and working at his hometown hospital—where he might run into her every day.

As the result of the rape a baby was conceived whom everyone assumed was Michael Horton, Jr. The only one who knew the truth was Laura's father-in-law, Tom Horton. When she and Mickey had gone to him for a sterility test, Mickey had checked out negative. He was incapable of fathering a child. But before he could learn the test results, Laura found that she was pregnant.

When Tom had called her in for an explanation, she'd learned about Mickey's test results and was forced by circumstance to reveal Bill's role.

Her first instinct had been to remain silent about the rape. Mickey was so proud of his impending fatherhood—the truth, she knew, could destroy him, for it would rob him of his child and his beloved brother at the same time. Also, Laura had dealt with enough families of rape cases to know that it would create in her husband's mind a doubt about her own complicity in the act itself. He would forever wonder whether it had indeed been rape. Since Laura and Bill had once been engaged, such a question would be inevitable.

Bill subsequently wrote to Laura, confessing his crime should she ever want to use it against him and promising never to hurt her again. This had reassured her, but Tom was another matter. As the father of both men, and the expectant grandfather of a baby sired by one and claimed by the other, he had to sort out what his best course was. Like Laura, his policy had always been to tell the truth whenever possible. In this case, he reluctantly went along with her request to remain silent.

Tom and Laura had come to this conclusion in the mistaken belief that Bill would never learn about his role in the fathering of Laura's baby.

Now everything was coming around full circle. Mickey already knew that Laura would be in charge of the investigation. Tom had told both of them that the state medical board would carefully examine her conclusions. There was no way she could tell her husband that she'd refused to help clear his devoted brother's name so that he could once again practice medicine. Unless she ran away, as Bill had once done, there was no way she would be allowed to forget him.

Running away seemed almost tempting. But she was a wife and a mother now, and had many troubled patients whose lives revolved around their visits to her office.

Just as Laura was reluctantly opening the envelope which contained her assignment regarding Bill's character report, his friend, Doug Williams, was being processed for release. After three years spent behind the walls of the state penitentiary Doug was counting the days. The tall, lean, long-limbed man had kept up his athletic physique by working out every day with the intensity of an Olympic contender. As he had told Bill Horton, "It's the only thing you can do around here that makes you feel good and doesn't get you in trouble."

Bill Horton, with just a few more months to go, found other outlets. He read a good deal, to keep up with his field, and his cell was filled with a wide assortment of medical journals. Every so often, Doug would pick one up and try to decipher the scientific jargon. Diseases he had never known existed popped out at him from illustrations more realistic than many a layman would like to see, even on an empty stomach. "You really have to be a true medical man or a weirdo to want to look at some of those pictures," Doug announced as he spied a particularly gory example and flung the magazine across the cell. "Ugh!"

"You really have to want to take up wrestling on TV or need to impress some pretty ladies to keep up with all that muscle flexing," Bill said in return.

In all their good-natured kidding, one subject was never mentioned: what careers they would pursue once they emerged from prison. Bill was only too aware that he might never be allowed to practice medicine again.

Doug, on the other hand, had no career or profession or anything else "legit" to which he wanted to return. He was a good accountant—self-taught—and salesman, and had occasionally served as a greeter at a hotel, a bouncer at a casino, and a bookie. But these were the sorts of jobs that led nowhere and in the long run got him into trouble with the law. He wanted to start over, with a clean slate. That required money. The easiest source of money, for Doug, would be wealthy women.

Topping the short list Doug had assembled was a certain Susan Martin who lived somewhere in the environs of Salem. That seemed as good a place to start as any. He was sure that Bill would have been more than glad to write on ahead to his family to treat his former cellmate to dinner and perhaps open a few doors. But that would also open a can of worms regarding his past, including the fact that he had been in prison in the first place.

No, Doug decided, all help seemed to come with strings attached or problems connected. On his last day, he affectionately cuffed Bill on the shoulder, promised to stay in touch, and jauntily walked out. Glancing at his even features, wavy brown hair, and huge blue eyes, any stranger would take him for a successful actor or athlete, tanned and terrific.

Julie had written "return to sender" on so many letters from Scott Banning that she even considered getting a rubber stamp made up. She had wanted all bonds permanently severed so that she and her son could live their lives free of uncomfortable memories, so the little boy had been returned to his natural mother without any allowance for visitation rights.

When a special delivery telegram arrived at her door in the hand of a uniformed messenger, she tipped the boy and ripped open the envelope assuming it was from her mother, who was traveling around the world and had friends scattered everywhere. First the name jumped out at her—Scott Banning—then the message, pleading with her to meet him at a place of her choice for a drink. He promised not to talk about visiting the baby or any of the other topics they had covered in court. He promised that this would be something else. Out of sheer curiosity, Julie assented.

She chose the clubhouse of her parents' old country club as the spot for their meeting, arranging it for the day of the state's interclub golf and tennis championship games, which were being held several counties away. There were good reasons for this choice. Since it was her "turf," it would be a place where Scott didn't belong, needed her permission to get in, and wasn't even allowed to pick up the tab. Also, they would probably be the only ones there that afternoon, but just to make sure of privacy, she reserved a well-placed alcove, a spot in which, it was rumored, many affairs had been conducted.

Arriving early, as befit a hostess, Julie noticed a green Ford parked outside the gate, with someone remarkably like Scott seated at the wheel, his face averted. Sure enough, as soon as she greeted the gatekeeper and instructed him to welcome her guest, the car revved its motor and pulled up behind her.

When the dining room captain ushered them to the legendary alcove, Julie was grateful that she had had the foresight to make arrangements ahead of time. It was privacy she was after. She wanted nothing else read into it, no problems, and most of all, no scenes. But now that the tension surrounding the trial was past, all the pleasant memories came back to her. Scott was essentially a good man, a caring man, the same man whom she had spoken with when she was pregnant, helpless, and bewildered. He was one half of the couple to whom she had entrusted her child. Memories came flooding back like a slide show of a family vacation: Scott and Janet befriending her; Scott and Janet telling her of how long they had waited for a baby, how hard they had tried to have one, how many lists they were on for adoption.

Julie remembered this nice-looking, idealistic man saying that he wanted to do things right. And from all the reports she'd heard, she had to admit that he had done the best he possibly could under very trying circumstances.

The captain himself brought their drinks and a tray of hors d'oeuvres, and then left them alone. Julie smiled in a neutral way, allowing Scott the time to get started and tell her what was on his mind.

His telegram had been correct. It *was* something that they had never discussed before and, yes, it surprised the hell out of her. He stared at his drink and put it aside. He took the big platter of hors d'oeuvres and placed it on another table. Then he looked her straight in the eye and said, "I would like you to consider marriage." She stared at him, nonplussed. "Marriage to me, that is," he added.

After a minute or two, Scott reached over for his drink and downed it in one, long swallow. Julie sat with her arms folded. Scott got up and paced. Looking for something to do, he picked up the platter of snacks and put it back on the table. Finally Julie said just one word: "Why?"

Scott worked his way around the question and spoke in fragments, hesitating every so often in an effort to phrase it attractively.

"You obviously don't love me," Julie said.

"I love your son, your flesh and blood. He reflects you and the man you chose to love. I'd say from the results that your choice was right, and you are going to be very proud of the boy. I'd like to be proud of him too. Besides, I am a widower living alone. I miss being married so much."

His voice broke on the last phrase. In any other circumstance, Julie would have reached over to comfort him. She recalled how she had felt when David died. No one had ever replaced him in her heart and she doubted that anyone ever could. Still, the question crept to the tip of her tongue and refused to be stifled.

"What about Susan?" she demanded.

Scott shrugged, attempting to indicate with the gesture that there was nothing more between them.

"You'll have to speak a little louder," Julie said sarcastically. "Shrugs just don't make it for me."

"Without Brad . . . I mean, David Junior . . ."

"I've been calling him Davy," Julie offered during the ensuing long pause.

"Without Davy," he continued, "life is over for me."

"And Susan?" Julie prompted.

"I stand by what I said. *With* Davy, *and* his mother, I think we could all have a good stab at finding happiness." He searched her face for a clue to her reaction.

Julie wanted some time to think about it. It was all so sudden and so surprising. It was the last thing she had expected the meeting to be about. A proposal! She wanted to dismiss it out of hand. Then she decided to take her time. She was in the driver's seat. There were no more deadlines for her. Let Scott sit by the phone and try to guess which way she would jump.

In the end, Julie took a long yellow pad and made a list of the pros and cons of her situation, and how marriage to Scott Banning would fit in. She had no particular aim in life as it was. They might grow fond of each other. The baby would regain the only father he had ever known. The list trailed down the page without inspiring a conclusion. Then Julie started doodling. When she looked at what she had done, she saw scrawled over and over again one word: Susan. She nodded. By marrying Scott, she could strike the crushing blow against the woman who had taken David from her by trickery. It was a way of evening the score.

One week to the day after their initial meeting, Julie pulled out the business card Scott had given to her and called him at work. "Yes," she said, matter-of-factly. "I'll marry you." His whoop of joy could almost have been heard without a phone. She was sure that as soon as she hung up, everyone in his office would be asking what *that* was about, and probably congratulating him. That part wasn't important. What she really wanted was to be a fly on the wall when he told Susan. She thought to herself, *Now that would be a scene to remember!*

Chapter Six

Afternoons of Passion

Several of the waitresses stood around the cash register, giggling. Their eyes were on the tall, good-looking man in the last booth who stared out of the plate-glass windows, oblivious to them all. He *had* to be an actor, they all agreed, but where had they seen him? Film or TV? No one that attractive, they thought, should be seated alone without anyone to interest or amuse him.

In the reflection in the window, Doug caught them watching him and heard the old familiar strains of giggling girls. It was a sound that had followed him since high school, daring him to do bigger, bolder, badder deeds until he outsmarted himself. Each time he got into trouble, one or another of those sweet young things would hide him, put him up for a night, lend him money, or lie for him. Even after a stretch in the state pen, he evidently hadn't lost his power to attract women. He knew that sooner or later one of them would approach him with a request for an autograph, certain that he was someone in show business.

It was a mixed blessing, he thought. Right now he would rather blend into the background, be a part of the scenery. He was reconnoitering Salem, taking its measure. He was also deciding on who he wanted to be. If there had been a chance meeting with some stranger-in-the-night, he could claim to be anyone the woman wanted him to be. But now he was trying a role on for size, one that must fit for a long time, a role that would win not only the attention but also the affection of Susan Martin.

Folded neatly by his plate was a copy of the daily newspaper. He would have studied it carefully for all the clues it could give him to Salem in general, but he was enjoying his first non rush, non hassle, civilized meal too much to interrupt it with business. He shuddered when he thought of the seamy cafeteria where he had shared all of his meals with hundreds of other inmates, each of them eating from compartmentalized Styrofoam trays with plastic utensils. He remembered the grayish meatloaf and canned vegetables consumed in an atmosphere that always exuded the odor of boiled cabbage.

Over his second cup of coffee, he read through the paper once for news items and notices of fraternal meetings, and a second time for advertisements. He remembered something that Bill Horton had said when he'd mentioned Susan, that she had been working for a local real estate firm when she came into her totally unexpected inheritance. He checked the advertisements until he found a name that rang a bell— Knowlton Realty. He politely brushed off the waitresses' questions with a "Who, me?" shrug, went into the men's room, and ran a comb through his luxuriant chestnut-brown hair. He checked the fit of his new off-the-rack tweed jacket and flannel slacks and decided that he would pass muster with a prospective employer.

One of the things men spoke about most in prison was how hard it was to find employment once they got out. What could they put on the application that wouldn't condemn them as untrustworthy? It was a real problem, but Doug thought that if he played his cards right, he might make it.

What a relief it was to step out into the sunlight with only his feet deciding which way he should go! Back in prison, once dinner was over, the men paraded to the day room where they all crowded around the single television set, battling over which show to watch.

When he entered Knowlton Realty, the secretary melted, as did the one saleswoman. Knowlton himself was less impressed, especially when he learned that the man seated across his desk was not a potential homeowner. Doug had noticed that one desk was empty in the outer office and wondered if Susan had not been replaced after she'd come into her money.

It was an offer Knowlton could not refuse. Doug wanted only the hardest plots of land and the most difficult houses, the ones which no one in the office had been able to move. He wished to try to sell them working only on commission. To make the offer even more attractive, he offered to work for a slightly lower than customary commission. With no payroll to enter on, no health plan or other paperwork involved, such a sales job was easier to get than a salaried position.

"What's the catch here?" Knowlton wanted to know. The man seemed too good to be true. His charm had gotten him into the firm's inner office. If that same charm could unload the firm's real "lemons," it might be worthwhile.

Doug leaned forward, relaxed, but wearing his most sincere, let-me-level-with-you look. "It's like this, sir. I've been an athlete most of my born days. That's how I got through school. Then, after a stint in the minor leagues playing baseball, I wandered around picking up coaching jobs at jerkwater high schools. It's about time I grew up and settled down."

Knowlton could immediately see the athlete in Doug. The way he carried himself, the outdoors look, the firm muscles—all of it spoke of clean living.

Doug watched the wheels go around in Knowlton's mind. He had purposely chosen that kind of background, knowing that it would be the hardest to trace, take the longest to get answers about, and offer the most dead ends. It was also the most believable.

"How's your golf?" Knowlton asked. Doug knew that he was in when he heard the question—the old man was picturing him at the country club with potential real estate purchasers.

"Golf's pretty good, tennis is a bit rusty," Doug replied.

He didn't dare to get any more specific than that. It had been years since he'd had a golf club in his hand, much less a tennis racquet. But he was in fighting trim from all of the workouts while he was in the slammer.

When Knowlton heard the word *tennis*, he nodded to himself, privately delighted. This big, rangy guy could cover a tennis court in a couple of bounding leaps. The number of deals that had been clinched over a friendly set of tennis! He could picture it now. If there was anything to find out, the sooner the better.

They gave Doug the empty corner desk and a phone which he had to share with someone until another line was put in. He spent the rest of the afternoon leafing through the book of "exclusives" and "semi-exclusives" and locating which of the homes pictured were to be assigned to him. Sooner or later, if it worked out, he would have to take courses toward a real estate license. But right now, Knowlton or one of his associates could cover that end of it for him.

By the second day, he had a couple of leads on potential buyers. More important, he had leads on Susan. That part was easy enough. He took the secretary to lunch and worked his way around to asking who used to occupy his desk. The starry-eyed secretary answered all his questions as fully as someone under hypnosis. It was his old charm pulling them in as always. Now all he needed was a little bit of luck. It came when he found out that Susan had used her old boss Knowlton as her real estate agent when she'd purchased her present home. Doug wondered if she still liked it, if she was interested in trading up, or perhaps just relocating. The rumor that the secretary had caught drift of was that Susan had been going with somebody. Doug felt that there was no time to lose.

There were the pills, a whole bottle of them, that Susan almost swallowed. There was the oven she would have turned on to asphyxiate herself, but it was electric. Then there was the car exhaust she only *thought* about. *If I survive everything that's coming down on me,* Susan said to herself, *no one will ever be able to hurt me again.*

Julie and Scott had married. The idea was so outlandish it would never have occurred to Susan in her wildest dreams—and Julie had often starred in Susan's wildest dreams! In every one of them was an avenging Julie, taunting her and torturing her for taking David away and tricking him into marriage.

Susan would be the first to agree that Julie was capable of exacting a hard, cruel form of revenge. But how could she have involved Scott? What was her diabolical hold over him? The baby, of course.

Scott was a kind man. He broke the news to her as gently as he could. "I would join my wife if I could, but Janet is beyond my reach forever," he'd said, slowly and with difficulty. "I *can* join my son, and I must. I spoke with Julie about it and she consented to marry me. Some day, Susan, perhaps you will find it in your heart to forgive me. My heart goes with my child. I have to follow the pull of my heart and try, with any luck, to raise my boy to be a young man the world can be proud of." And that had been that.

Sooner or later, Susan would have to take some action. She'd have to clean the house or sell it or both. She'd have to pull herself together. The first step was a long, hot bath and a long session brushing out her bushy blond hair. Slipping into a pair of jeans and one of Scott's shirts, she searched for her nail polish. That would be one way to pass a half-hour or so—giving herself a manicure. But her nails were bitten down to the quick. Tossing aside her manicure case, she walked downstairs to check on the mail, when the bell rang.

It sure isn't the mailman, Susan told herself when she caught sight of Doug standing diffidently on her front steps. He mentioned the familiar words *Knowlton Realty* and she agreed to let him in.

"So there I was seated at what was your old desk in the real estate office and . . ."

Susan waited politely for him to continue. Doug grew puzzled. This wasn't the way things usually worked. When he laid on his charm *that* thick, a pause would be an invitation for the lady he was addressing to rush in to complete the sentence.

"I thought I'd stop by and say hello. Now that you've become a customer, maybe you might think of trading up, or selling or . . . well, you know."

He's a charmer, all right, Susan thought. *He's trying his number on me.* At any other time it might have worked, but right now she felt anesthetized.

She leaned forward and asked slyly, "What would *you* like me to do? Do you know something about the real estate market that I don't know? Like, is it a good time to sell or a good time to buy or a good time to stand pat and stay put?" Before he could answer, she pushed on. "Or maybe you know something I don't know about my personal life that makes it a good time to move?"

Doug hadn't been in town long enough to pick up any gossip in *that* direction. But Susan sure didn't look to him like a lady in love waiting around for whoever it was to carry her off on a honeymoon. The rumor the secretary had heard was that she was going with someone. From her manner, it looked as though that was no longer the case.

Doug leaned back on the sofa and stretched his long legs, shrugged, and gave his practiced approximation of a shy smile. "Lady, give me a break, willya? I'm sure that when you were in my position at that old gray, metal desk, sharing a phone and trying to sell those Godawful houses to reluctant buyers, you worked pretty hard at it too."

This bit of sweet talk softened Susan up enough to perk some coffee and break open the cookies. Seeing that Doug was earnest about picking up real estate tips, she shared what she knew, explaining that she'd really only worked as a receptionist. The afternoon ended with Susan promising to drop into town for dinner later in the week. She surprised herself by adding that if she decided to sell her place, she'd consider giving him first crack at the sale.

Doug boned up on the romantic night spots during the following days. He chose a new French restaurant on top of the Professional Building that had the lighting and atmosphere sought after by lovers. Susan enjoyed the effort he was expending and found the food surprisingly good. Knowing what he must be making as a commission-only salesman, she had to hold herself back from offering to cover the check.

Looking across the table at Doug by candlelight, she could understand something of the magnetic allure of the man. What she *couldn't* understand was why he wasn't turning her on. She could picture herself walking down the street with him, dancing at a night spot, or just being in his company in public and driving every other woman around crazy with jealousy. Even Julie.

Doug reached out for her hand with a look of tenderness in his eyes. Susan didn't pull away. Rather, she patted his hand with a gesture of innocuous friendliness. He seemed so puzzled by his inability to get through to her, that she took pity on him. "Doug, I want you to know here and now that I think you are one of the most attractive, charming, charismatic guys I have ever met." She could see that he was pleased by that, and so she continued. "At any other time in my life . . ." She let her voice trail off so that he could fill in what was unsaid.

"What's wrong with right now?" Doug asked.

A thousand things rushed through Susan's mind. The answer was none of Doug's business, but *she* had introduced the topic and phrased it in such a way that his question was a natural one. She couldn't fault him for asking. Finally she said, "Right now, I am emotionally numb. Too many things happened to me over too short a period of time." She could see Doug's eyes light up with the challenge. A chance to soothe a troubled spirit would be too exciting to pass up. But why? Surely she wasn't the only woman in Salem. Even in her most self-confident mood, Susan never considered herself to be a world-class beauty. And yet he sought her out.

Once again Doug asked, "Well, what *is*

wrong about right now? The best way to forget your troubles might be to go with the flow. And baby, I'll steer your little boat just as long and hard as you let me."

My God, what a line! Susan thought. Any other woman would be panting with desire at this very moment. Even Julie. Why was this man wasting such stunning lines and glorious looks on her? Then she remembered his job at Knowlton's. No one could work there for five minutes without being completely filled in by the secretary on the private lives of every employee and ex-employee. Buy the woman a lunch and she would open all the files to a cute guy like Doug.

Again Susan's thoughts raced as she gazed at her escort through the romantic glow of the flickering candles. What tale would be as worth the telling as that of the young woman who sat at the gray metal corner desk working for peanuts in a real estate office . . . a young woman who kissed off the job when she came into an unexpected inheritance, and then turned around and bought a house from the same firm she had slaved for! Doug might be complimenting her on her bright, blond hair or perky looks or sexy figure, but the figures that grabbed his attention were probably in her bankbook. For the first time she realized that she was being courted for her money!

She pleaded a headache and asked to be taken home early. She had a great deal to think about. She knew that Doug would be a good man to have in her corner if she played her cards right. It was toward that end that she promised to call him soon to let him know that she was feeling better.

By the next day, she had everything worked out in her mind and invited Doug over for lunch later in the week. Dinner would have had too suggestive a ring to it, but lunch could hold out hopes for him of a long, lazy afternoon. Instead, she had a deal to propose.

Over the platter of assorted sandwiches, they chatted about the real estate business and the leads Doug was pursuing. Then, while she was pouring coffee, Susan said casually, "There's a very attractive young woman I'd like you to meet."

Doug spilled his coffee and almost dropped the cup. This was something he had heard off and on since adolescence, but the words had always come from middle-aged women who wanted to fix him up with their daughters. It just didn't figure as something Susan would say. He decided that he must have misunderstood her and asked her to repeat it.

"You heard me right," Susan said, still smiling, but with a strange intensity that seemed at odds with what she was saying. Then she added slyly, looking him straight in the eye, "And *she* has more money than *I* do."

Now everything was beginning to make sense. He was still to learn the details, but he now understood that Susan had his number. She almost said it in so many words—"Your game is money and I have a business deal for you."

Anticipating his next question, she then added, "And there's nothing illegal involved in anything I'm going to suggest. Not if you play it cool, that is." She cleared away the dishes and handed him a pad and a pen. Then she began dictating in the manner of Old Man Knowlton giving real estate assignments.

"Name—Julie Banning. She's exactly my age, a little shorter and slighter, with long straight brown hair. Many men seem to find her attractive. Until recently, she was Julie Olson. She just married my next-door neighbor, Scott Banning."

Doug remembered the girl at Knowlton's saying that Susan had been "going with someone." Now he realized that the someone must have been Scott Banning. Thinking of how quickly Banning must have shifted his attentions from Susan to this Julie, Doug mumbled almost to himself, "Wow! It must have been a whirlwind courtship." Susan nodded.

He got up and paced around the room. He was beginning to think life had been much simpler back at the state pen. The food wasn't as good and the day room was crowded, but you knew where you stood with people. Here was an attractive, lonesome young widow. What was she doing hiring him to seduce another man's wife?

"I can really make it worth your while," Susan said. "It will be a lot easier than trying to unload some third-rate real estate on second-rate people who end up not buying anyway. It will also be more profitable by a long shot."

"It *is* a long shot," Doug snapped back. "The lady married Banning of her own free will. She's undoubtedly in her right mind." Susan nodded. "And they're barely out of their honeymoon phase." Again Susan nodded. "So how do *I* get off trying to come on to a lady in love with her husband?"

"She's *not* in love with him. At least I'm positive that she wasn't when she agreed to marry him. She had an illegitimate baby and he was a convenient second hand father."

Doug, who had been illegitimate himself, thought it sounded very decent of Julie to find a father for the kid. But business was business. "It's not going to be easy," he said.

"If it was, I wouldn't be prepared to pay you scads of money to do it. I'd just let nature take its course. That marriage was not made in heaven. Sooner or later it's going to fall apart at the seams. You're just going to speed up the process." Doug looked doubtful. Susan reached out and patted him on the shoulder. "You're a first-rate salesman. I know you'll make out just fine."

When Doug headed back to town, he carried a sizable check in his wallet as a down payment, and instructions to head for Blessington's Department Store to be completely outfitted—two pairs of shoes, a couple of suits and slacks and sport jackets and ties. "The all-silk British kind," Susan had said. "Julie can tell the difference." All of this was to go on her account.

He decided to keep his job. It gave him a sense of legitimacy, a reason to be in town. Besides, as a commission-only outside salesman, he had no one to answer to for time off in the service of courtship and seduction.

Doug remembered his first cellmate upstate. He had run elaborate schemes and scams for years before he was caught. In the course of advising Doug, the older man had stressed the importance of research. "When you hit a new town, check into the local paper," he had said. "If there are names to look up, you should sometimes go as far back as someone's birth announcement."

Doug spent several days in the library going over back issues of the local paper. He traced Julie's history through her parents, Ben and Addie Olson, read Ben's obituary, and saw that Susan was indeed telling him the truth. Julie Olson Banning must be worth a helluva lot of money. More recently, Scott and Julie seemed to have taken an active role in the local country club, on both the golf course and the tennis courts.

This time when Doug requested a few minutes of Old Man Knowlton's time, he looked almost too successful for his job. Knowlton spotted the tasseled loafers, the silk socks, and the fine wool trousers as Doug leaned back in the chair and crossed his long legs. The tie Doug wore was of a better quality than Knowlton's own—Liberty silk, from London. None of this wardrobe could have come from real estate sales. Doug's file lay open on Knowlton's desk, and it looked pretty static. He expected as much from the tired old losers he had assigned to the young man. Perhaps he had come in to tender his resignation. Knowlton would have expected as much. He gestured to the file. "Not much action, I see," he observed. "Pretty slim pickings?"

Doug nodded. "But I haven't given up," he said. "I thought that if I invested in a wardrobe and polished up my golf and tennis, you'd give me a shot at a better class of clientele." Then, while Knowlton's mouth hung open in surprise that Doug wasn't handing in his keys, Doug continued. "I'm kind of new here. Is there some sort of country club where I might meet *our* sort of customers, Mr. Knowlton?"

Before the day was out, Knowlton had called up the club and arranged for a long-term guest membership in Doug's name. The membership was on the firm. The golf clubs and tennis gear which Doug later picked up in Blessington's sporting goods department were put on Susan Martin's account.

Doug spent the next several days walking the golf course and practicing teeing off. His muscles responded as if he had played his last game yesterday. Tennis was a little harder. The wrist motion was almost the opposite of Ping-Pong, which he had played almost incessantly in prison. A few strong sessions against a practice backboard and then one with the tennis pro, and Doug felt ready.

And just in time. Several events listed on the club calendar for the weekend were sure to attract one or both of the Bannings. Doug's one fear had always been of being caught unprepared. Now he felt ready to meet and beat the town's social class at their own country club games. "Julie Olson Banning, here I come, ready or not!"

Doug stood at the clubroom bar fiddling with his vodka and tonic, waiting for Julie to enter. He had watched her earlier on the tennis court and thought he had caught her eye once or twice. This was unusual in itself, for the young woman kept her eye very much on the ball, winning both the sets he'd watched. He wondered which of the other onlookers was her husband, until he heard one of the staff page her to call her husband at home.

When he saw her enter the room, Doug gave a nod and a slight wave of approval. As she approached, he held out his hand and introduced himself.

"So *you're* the new member who's been giving the tennis pro quite a runaround. I understand that you're pretty good."

Doug switched to his aw-gee-whiz look of modesty, but didn't say anything. On the tennis court, Julie was a bundle of energy and grace under pressure. Now, seated beside him on a high bar stool, she looked fragile and vulnerable, with huge, haunting eyes, perfect features, and flawless creamy-white skin. Her lustrous dark shoulder-length hair was pulled back by expensive-looking combs on each side. She smiled. Doug thought she was gorgeous.

Julie persisted. "Look, I didn't say that to compliment you. I'm asking for confirmation that you know how to swing a racquet and drive a serve. My mixed-doubles partner just canceled out and I'm looking for a replacement for this afternoon. What do you say?"

After that it was easy. They won the set, almost acing their opponents. A stranger would have guessed that they had grown up playing mixed doubles together. They performed as gracefully as Fred Astaire and Ginger Rogers, with the tennis court as their dance floor. Anticipating each other's movements, they whirled about, returning the impossible cannonball serve, and serving the unreturnable killer ball. A crowd gathered.

Afterward they were toasted and Doug was officially welcomed to the club. It was actually more attention than he wanted for his illicit purposes, but he knew that word would get back to Old Man Knowlton, and that could always be a plus. His job was his ticket and he wasn't making many sales. This way, he could be said to be working on long-range plans.

After the celebration, they each went their separate ways, but not before Julie suggested another tennis date for Monday. It made sense. Weekday mornings were always quiet at the club, Doug had observed that the week before. As much as tennis might be on Julie's mind, discretion was in both of their interests.

When Julie arrived Monday, Doug was waiting for her, his lanky frame slouched against the steel fencing of the red clay center tennis court. This was the most sought-after court of all, for red clay was expensive to keep up and best when you were first to use it. Doug and Julie put in their bid for mornings every day for the next two weeks.

Each day, they left the courts, showered, and drove off, presumably in separate directions. By the second day, however, they had arranged to rendezvous in a restaurant out of town. Julie was embarrassed about their elaborate plans to meet secretly. "After all, it's merely extending a good, healthy friendship beyond the game itself, isn't it? I mean . . . if this wasn't such a small town, we wouldn't even bother—right?"

He watched her bite into the olive with her strong white teeth. She held her martini glass with long scarlet-nailed fingers that seemed at variance with her athletic stance at the club. These were graceful hands that one couldn't begin to picture walloping a ball out of reach of an opponent.

This time, Doug couldn't think of an answer. He kept quiet because he felt so stupid. It was not to be believed—he had fallen completely in love with Julie and the effect was overpowering. He thought that if he opened his mouth to speak he would not be able to hold in his emotions. He looked as moonstruck as a high school kid.

It took Julie a little longer. The next day, as they were lunching in a plush dining room where their red banquette was almost surrounded by mirrors, she caught Doug's reflection at an odd angle. She gasped and held her breath. It could have been David Martin! His strong hands had the same squared-off nails as he lifted his glass. His jawbone had the same lean line and jaunty angle.

By the end of the week they had located a quaint out-of-town guest house in which to spend the afternoons. Their rear bedroom had a separate entrance, which they carefully did not enter together. When they made love, it was with an earth-shattering passion that neither had ever experienced before. Their bodies seemed to have known each other forever, and the ecstasies they found in that little guest house surprised and at times almost overwhelmed them.

But they both had cause to feel guilty about the affair, and they were concerned to keep it secret. Julie, for her part, considered her son as well as her new husband. Her marriage to Scott had been preceded by a proposal as cool as a business arrangement. Scott was interested in the baby, first and foremost. True, an affection had grown up between them, even a love of sorts. But it was not strong enough to satisfy the burning passion that ignited Julie's life and seemed destined to go on and on like an eternal flame.

What would this do to the baby? Little Davy had been through so many changes in his short life that he needed some sense of stability. That was what Julie's Aunt Laura and Grandma Alice had tried to tell her months ago. At the time, no one had been able to get through to her. She was a bundle of despair and revenge. Now, suffused by an all-encompassing love, she saw the entire world differently. At least for the present, they must maintain absolute secrecy.

With Doug the problem went much deeper. He wanted to throw back in Susan's face every cent she had given him. He wanted to undo everything shady he had ever done in his life. He wanted Julie to be proud of him, really proud—to accept his questionable past and believe in a bright, promising future for the two of them— together. He wanted to be the best real estate salesman that Old Man Knowlton had ever seen.

In the meantime, until he could figure out how all these things could be accomplished, he concurred with Julie about secrecy. They stopped playing at the club. He used mornings and evenings to follow up real estate leads. Afternoons were reserved for just the two of them.

Chapter Seven
Love in the Sun

After her fling with Mario had ended, Addie mooned around Naples and then Rome, touring the Vatican, the Colosseum, and sampling some of the many museums. Still feeling aimless and a little sad, she rented a car and drove along the Mediterrean coast through Livorno, Monte Carlo, and Nice. Nothing helped. She just felt fat and tired.

The health spa was on a tiny island off Majorca. It was the only place on the island where one could eat. That was the way they planned it. If you were very rich and wanted to lose weight, you'd have to swim to get any pizza or pastries or even a long loaf of ordinary French bread.

The schedule was as strict as that of a prison. Up at six. So many lengths to swim in the pool, so many laps to run around the track, so many push-ups and knee bends and minutes on the stationary bicycle. The instructors were mostly women. Those who were men didn't seem to like women, which was just as well. Addie worked out so thoroughly that at the end of the day all she could do was crawl into bed and dream about food.

At "graduation," she had lost all her excess weight and acquired the most thorough and complete tan of her life. She looked and felt years younger. Once again, she was ready to take on the world of men.

The tiny plane's first stop was Majorca. With no particular plans in mind, Addie got off, while the others continued on. The little hotel was elegant and just a few steps from the sea. There, on the beach, she met Arne.

"My dear lady," he said, brushing his damp hair out of his eyes and shaking his blond head in wonder at her question. "My dear—Addie, in Norway we learn English when we learn our own language. It is more than a second tongue." He leaned over and gazed into her eyes so closely that she saw herself reflected in his. "English is a language we know . . . intimately." There was no mistaking his meaning: He wanted to know Addie as well as he knew English.

Arne had left Norway because he hated the cold. The very tall, very fair-skinned and handsome Scandinavian amused and entertained Addie with tales of the grim winters of his childhood and the eternal summers he had chosen to follow all over the world ever since.

"A Norwegian cowboy?" she asked.

"Where?"

"In Argentina. They have more cattle than you have ever seen in your life and when it is winter where you come from, it is summer there."

"Surely you're not still in the cowboy business," Addie said, hoping that the answer would be no and that this Norse god belonged to a respectable class of society.

Arne was a travel agent. He was still learning the business, so he worked for someone else. "But some day . . . " Addie loved the way his already sunny face lit up over dinner as he told her about his plans and dreams. Some day, he would have his own travel agency, dealing only in sunny climates. He might even set up an office in Rome, Cairo, or . . .

In answer to his question, Addie told him the name of her hometown.

"Fine," he beamed. "Also an office in Salem. Would you like that?"

"Our winters can get pretty bad," Addie teased.

"Only in summer then. Salem in summer —I'd say it sounds like the title of a song. Like 'April in Paris.' What do you think?"

Addie thought that he was too good to be true. The lines were spoken with a silky smoothness. But that may have been her imagination acting up—maybe it was just the allure of the rich American widow for a struggling young travel agent.

Deep down, though, she knew she was amusing and full of fun. That had been her stock-in-trade since high school: while others vied to be prettiest, she was always thought to have the best personality. It won her Ben, and it proved invaluable to him during endless dinners and formal evenings spent entertaining clients.

Arne was a far easier conquest than Ben had been. *More fun, too,* she thought. "Come," Arne had said, "let me show you my favorite spots, just a few of them."

So they wined, and they dined, and they danced till the small hours. And when all of Arne's favorite spots had closed down, Addie took him by the arm and squeezed up nice and close. "Now," she whispered in her huskiest voice, "let me show you some of *my* favorite spots." This time he left all the details to her, and whatever language barrier remained between them was finally lifted. . . .

They arrived in Athens in time for the wine festival. Arne bought them each a wine bucket and they went from one wine seller's stall to another, tasting and discussing the vintages like seasoned connoisseurs. Then, to Arne's view of heaven: a long cruise through the Greek islands. It was toward the tail end of the cruise that Addie started feeling poorly.

"It's probably just a bug I picked up," she said, ready to dismiss anything that might get in the way of fun and romance. But it continued back in Athens when they visited the historic ruins and saw a Greek play at the same ancient amphitheater in which, in all probability, it was first performed. Addie tried to shake off the all-pervasive feeling of fatigue—she'd be damned if she'd let this golden god think her too old or too slow. She gripped his hand and smiled up at him as the play began.

Whatever it was about, there was a huge Greek chorus divided into male and female sections. The men swayed in their long white tunics and flowing beards; the women wore long white gowns. Together they sang, moaned, and screamed, as is customary in Greek tragedy. Addie began to sway with them. Without understanding a word of Greek, she thought they seemed to be saying, "Addie, go home. You are a stranger. You've been here too long. Addie, go home."

She fainted.

When she came to, she was back in her hotel room with a Greek doctor chattering away in his native tongue to a worried Arne. When Arne finally looked down and noticed that her eyes were open, he reassured her with a smile. "He can't say for sure. Some sort of bug or virus you must have picked up. Certainly, it's nothing life-threatening, or even very serious. I didn't want to check you into an Athens hospital without your O.K., darling."

Addie sat up and shook her head. "No, not here, please!" During her years abroad with Ben, whenever anyone was sick, they flew directly to the American Hospital in Paris. She told Arne that was where she wanted to go. Right now. Then she saw his face fall.

The problem was that he was already off schedule. Part of his work had been to check out tourist facilities throughout the Greek islands and then go on to Spain and Portugal before heading even further away. He had so enjoyed showing Athens to her, but . . .

"Don't be silly, Arne. I don't want you to place your job in jeopardy."

"It already is." He smiled sadly. "That is, unless I get on the stick immediately." Whenever Arne used slang, it amused Addie. It sounded so strange, with just a tinge of a Norwegian accent. "But first I have to see you safely to Paris and to the hospital there."

Addie shook her head decisively. "No, my dear. The doctor seems to feel that I am perfectly able to make the trip by myself."

"But when will I see you? You will rejoin me on the coast of Portugal, I hope."

Addie made no promises. Right now she longed more for the American doctors than for any lover. She took the first flight out of Athens, kissing Arne and leaving him standing at the gate, a head taller and blonder than anyone else in the crowd.

Once in Paris, Addie grabbed a cab to the hotel. She told the driver to wait for her, checked in, and then rushed to the American Hospital. A series of slides and chest thumps and standard procedures went on in the calmly efficient manner she remembered from her childhood. The smiling, competent manner of the staff soothed her fears. She could have been back at her father's hospital in Salem.

When her doctor came in with the final verdict, he said, "Relax. It's over. Whatever you picked up has definitely run its course. I see from your Athens records that you were quite feverish. No more."

"When can I leave, Doctor?"

He shrugged and asked, "Leave the hospital or leave for the States?"

"Both," Addie heard herself say without realizing what she was saying until it was out of her mouth.

"You can leave the hospital today. But I suggest that you take it easy for a few days and see me once more before you get back on a plane. You want your family to see you in tiptop shape, don't you?"

And boy, was he right, Addie thought after she got back to the hotel. She wanted to be not only healthy, but as stunningly attired as any wealthy Parisian. She wanted to show Salem what *haute couture* meant: the creations of the leading designers of high-fashion clothing in the world.

Since the capital of the fashion world was right here in Paris, Addie called around, arranging appointments at the current showings. The widow of the international banker Ben Olson was readily accommodated. The slimming exercises and the diet had resulted in svelte dimensions, made even more so by the recent bout of illness.

"Madame!" Each of the French designers shrieked, "You look *magnifique!* And at least twenty years younger than the last time we met. If you didn't tell me, I would have guessed that you were your own daughter!"

It was all music to her ears. With a practiced eye she selected just the right outfits, matching them up with handmade shoes and handbags. She did everything efficiently now that she was feeling better. Two hours each afternoon she napped, and every night she retired early with a book. After two or three pages, she would fall asleep. One week of shopping and watching her health, and she was back at the American Hospital for her checkup.

Her doctor gave her a clean bill of health and celebrated with her over some wine, cheese, and croissants. Mixing the breakfast roll with the late afternoon foods was a habit of Americans abroad, and Addie saw it as still another sign that her return trip was long overdue. A kiss on the cheek from her Frenchified American doctor, then back to the hotel to check out, and she was on the plane for the good old U.S. of A.

Once she was aboard, she saw, crammed into her purse with the hotel receipt, some mail. It was a letter from Arne. He certainly seemed to have a better command of spoken English than written English. It was written in pencil and contained amusingly awful mistakes and misspellings. The gist of it was that he would like to visit her, to discuss opening a tourist bureau in Salem.

Addie was relieved that he didn't mention a date for the visit. Indeed, he listed a series of return addresses, fitted around his business trips. It seemed to encompass a year's itinerary. It was clear that he didn't want to miss her return letter.

Addie held the letter in her hand for a moment, began to crumple it up, and then smoothed it out again. Perhaps she'd take another journey some day and call on Arne. One thing she felt sure of: It was hard to see Arne fitting into the life she pictured for herself in Salem. Still, she reminded herself, stranger things can happen.

She sipped her second martini and reached for another glossy American magazine. It was a long time since she'd been in touch with what was going on back home.

Chapter Eight

The Shadow of Suspicion

Julie was beside herself with anguish. Her increasingly complicated life was rapidly becoming unmanageable. Up until now, she had amazed herself and others with her businesslike way of cutting through red tape and accomplishing whatever she had set out to do. Her Uncle Mickey might not approve of everything she did, her grandparents might have suggested other ways of handling certain matters, but no one could call her inefficient. When it came to taking care of business, she was pure Olson.

Alice Horton watched her grandchild bake cookies in the kitchen and marveled at how time had flown. Now Julie had a child of her own and a husband, in that order. To the world, she was a sophisticated young woman. To her grandma, she was still a tearful little girl.

"Of all times to come barging in," Julie

sniffled, waving Addie's telegram by the edge as if it were likely to go up in flames. "Just as we were all getting our lives in order."

Addie had cabled Julie to expect her within the week. She would be staying in the tower suite of the St. Francis for the time being. The tone of her long, expensive cablegram suggested that she had much to catch up with, and couldn't wait to see everyone and settle back in where she "truly belonged."

Alice patted Julie's shoulder reassuringly and said, "It isn't as if your mother wants to move in with you. Of all my children, Addie was always the most independent. Even more than any of the boys."

"Yeah," Julie pouted. "Independent, bossy, self-centered, selfish, know-it-all, and Daddy is always right." They both thought of Ben— Ben, who had left such an indelible mark on the emotions of his wife and daughter.

"Half of what you're describing is your father, you know," Alice pointed out. "Addie may be a great deal different now that he's gone."

"She never stood up for me," Julie sobbed, "not once in my entire life!"

"Because your father insisted that the two of them stick together," Alice said. "He made her take an oath always to tell him the truth, never to hide anything, and never to contradict him in public."

"*I* was 'public'?" Julie demanded. "I was his *own child!*"

Alice shook her head with frustration. How could she explain that complicated man to his own daughter, when she didn't completely understand him herself? "Your mother never said that much about it. Just little slips here and there. What it amounted to was an attitude the two of them struck against the world." She saw Julie's puzzled look and tried to clarify her words. "There were no exceptions."

"Why didn't my mother ever say no to my father?" Julie asked.

"Because that was part of the bargain, the promise. They were very faithful to each other at a time when divorces were going on all around them. You've got to hand it to them. In their own way, on their own terms, Ben and Addie had a good, solid marriage."

"Then why did they bother with any kids in the first place?" said Julie, with bitterness. "Just because it would look good on Dad's résumé or in a newspaper interview?"

Alice adjusted the dial, slid in the cookie sheets, and closed the oven door. Then she poured the tea and sat down opposite her granddaughter.

"I am sure that Ben loved you very deeply in his own way."

"As long as he *got* his own way," Julie retorted sullenly.

"We don't often have completely free choices in life," Alice said. "We certainly aren't free to pick our own parents. There are tales I could tell you about friends of mine, and tales Grandpa and your uncles could tell you about the people they deal with. Doctors and lawyers learn the ugly side of very attractive families. Next to some, your childhood was nothing to complain about."

Julie smiled through her tears. "I could always run to you and Grandpa," she said, rising from her chair and reaching to hug her grandmother. The two women held each other for a moment.

"Please give your mother a chance," Alice went on. "You can never be sure how much was her doing and how much was in response to your father's demands. She's my child, you know. Let's all start again with a clean slate."

"Maybe you and Grandpa could see her when she arrives. Scott and I could take the baby away for the weekend and . . ."

This time Alice put her foot down. "You've had plenty of advance notice. It would be an insult to your mother, whom you haven't seen in so long, and it would put a terrible strain on your entire future relationship."

In the end, they reached a compromise. Alice would have Mickey and Laura for dinner, together with Scott and Julie. Addie would be meeting a new sister-in-law and a new son-in-law at the same time, and the heat would be off Julie during the grand reunion. Once the ice was broken, everyone would be on their own.

Julie thought about it for a minute and then agreed. The lines left her face and she looked like a kid again. But unlike the youngster who, a few short years ago, waited around the kitchen until the cookies were done, she glanced at her watch. She mentioned an important appointment, grabbed her jacket, kissed Alice, and was off. Once in her car, she adjusted the rear-view mirror to check her makeup, sprayed on some perfume, and headed for her rendezvous with Doug.

"What's the matter, honey?" Doug asked, tenderly. The question echoed Scott's earlier in the day, when she snapped at him at breakfast and showed the same concern. It drove her up the wall.

"Please allow me to have *my* moods and I'll allow you yours," Julie retorted. This was something that would have made no sense to Scott, because he *had* no moods—or at least he never revealed any to Julie. He was a good, decent, uncomplicated man, an ideal father. In his own way, he was also a good provider. He insisted that she invest her inheritance and let him cover all household expenses. His construction business was growing slowly and he had long-range plans that included adding an "and son" to the company name. Julie worked out a compromise whereby she paid for the second car and any "extravagances." The latter included Carmen, the baby's nurse, who allowed Julie the free time she needed.

"A penny for your thoughts," Doug whispered. They were in their bedroom at the guest house. Having made love, they lay now side by side on the rumpled bedclothes, enjoying the drowsy languor that follows intense passion. But there was still a tension in Julie, and Doug had noticed it.

"Guess," she responded, more to give herself a chance to think of a good answer than for any other reason.

"You're thinking how much you love me," Doug replied. He lifted her head by placing a hand on each side, and gently kissed her. Then he caressed and stroked her, until she began to relax.

"Do you feel a little better now?" he asked softly.

"Nothing was wrong with me to begin with," Julie snapped.

"There you go again. Nothing is *ever* wrong with you as far as *I'm* concerned," Doug answered lightly, kissing her as if to emphasize the point. "It's just that I hate to see you worried. You look as if you had seen a ghost."

Unspoken between them was Scott's name. Doug was sure that Julie's husband knew nothing about them. She was very careful. But one could never be *too* sure. More important to him was the everpresent concern that Susan would spill the beans. Now that he genuinely loved Julie, he wanted to build that love to a mutuality that could transcend any gossip or slurs.

At times he wanted to blurt out to Julie the pact he had made with Susan. He wanted to put it behind them so that they could build a life together, united by nothing but the truth and their love for each other.

But Doug never trusted his own good luck. From his troubled childhood on, he had met with so many bad breaks and disappointments that he didn't dare take any chance with Julie's love. It was the one good thing in his life. The longer he could hold on to it, the more secure he would be.

"Good old American cooking," Addie chortled, "I can't begin to tell you how welcome it is." She gave Alice a look of appreciation, well aware that every eye in the room was on her.

"I assumed that all that fancy food in Paris and Italy would have jaded you to things like Mom's apple pie," Mickey said. Jaded or not, he had never seen his older sister look so stunning. She seemed to have lost years, and might even be taken for his *younger* sister. He couldn't wait to get Laura's first impressions of her. Having a psychiatrist for a wife, he reflected, definitely had its advantages. As Laura met each member of the family, she began to see the Horton clan as a vast jigsaw puzzle. She was able to sort out the neurotic tendencies, trace mannerisms, and generally gain insights which Mickey could have never gotten on his own.

Earlier, when Addie and Julie had greeted each other, Julie had skillfully averted her head just enough so that both women kissed the air. Addie bided her time. There would be plenty of opportunity to sort out old problems, resolve tensions, and get rid of grudges. It all depended on Julie.

Two surprises greeted Addie. The first was the stunner of a wife her brother Mickey had chosen for himself. Laura was a poised, self-assured beauty. She approved of her brother's choice and was happy for him.

Addie's second surprise wasn't quite so pleasant. Scott Banning was something else again. If he were placed in a roomful of middle-class men, he would be the last one Addie would have guessed might appeal to Julie. He was "Mr. Average": good, sweet, earnest, and probably dull as dish water. He would never become very rich or powerful, and she sensed no smoldering intensity or panache. She could have pictured her daughter choosing a member of the Hell's Angels sooner than Scott.

Before the evening broke up, arrangements were made for Addie to visit little David during the week. She had not been pleased to learn that she was a grandmother at this stage of her life, especially now that she was single and in the market for an attractive, vibrant, youthful "Mr. Right" of her own. She took her brother's teasing with practiced nonchalance, but all the same, it irritated her.

It was just as she was almost imperceptibly wincing that she noticed Julie watching her closely. She said to herself, *So, Julie thinks she has my number. Well, we'll see.*

Two days later, when Addie was shopping in Blessington's, she caught sight of Julie seated in her car outside the rear entrance.

A moment later, a tall, good-looking man dashed out of a building across the way, opened the door on the passenger side, got in and kissed her. The clinch lasted for a full half-minute before Julie put the car into gear. Addie stood open-mouthed as she watched them pull away.

At the club the following day, she again caught sight of the tall mystery man as she was waiting to tee off on the practice green. He had just returned from the tennis courts with another man, and they were laughing and joking on the way to the shower. She didn't want to make too much of it or indicate any unusual curiosity; but one of the stewards thought he knew who she was casually referring to.

"Oh, that's Mr. Williams. He's kind of new here. But he's one heck of an athlete."

The bartender was able to fill in the first name—Doug. She could have undoubtedly learned a good deal more, but not without attracting attention. On a hunch, she visited Blessington's later in the week, at the same hour, and stood at the same window overlooking the rear entrance. Once more Julie sat waiting in the car and once more Doug Williams rushed over and embraced her. Then the two of them drove away.

It was her responsibility as a mother, Addie told herself, to find out what was going on.

For some months, Buck Harris slept on the couch in his office to save on rent. He dodged debt collectors and fell behind on his utility bills. But his phone bill was always up to date, as was his answering service. Phone calls were the life blood of his business. And in good times or bad, the local Yellow Pages always carried a discreet ad advising would-be clients that he was available to serve them in all kinds of investigations of a personal nature.

Quite some time had gone by since Buck had produced the information which enabled Julie Olson to nail Susan Martin in the adoption proceeding. The files were now in the "inactive" cabinet. When Buck got a call from a Mrs. Olson, the name rang a bell. He checked out Julie's files to ascertain that she was a *Miss* Olson. He wondered if they were related.

Addie took one horrified look at the long dark corridor on the third floor of the Newspaper Building and almost turned on her heel to leave. The hallway was dingy, the linoleum was curling at the edges, the entire atmosphere reminded her of an old black-and-white movie starring Humphrey Bogart or James Cagney, with the words *Private Eye* somewhere in the title.

The location had only one thing going for it, Addie decided. She could enter, conduct her business and depart, assured of not running into anyone in her social set.

Mrs. Olson looked nothing like the Julie Olson Buck remembered. She was easily a decade-and-a-half older. As he waltzed her to the one unbroken chair facing the desk, he caught the aroma of fifty-dollar-an-ounce French perfume and the reflection of a spotlight-sized square-cut diamond which almost obscured a band of smaller diamonds. Third finger, left hand. The lady was *not* a divorcee. She was either actively married or widowed. Chances are, Buck deduced, that the lady could not only pay her bill, but buy and sell him, the Newspaper Building, and possibly half of Salem.

Addie allowed Buck to light her French cigarette for her. When he then lit his cigar, Addie's cigarette had the stronger, more pungent odor. Then she got straight to the point. His assignment: to find out everything he could about one Douglas Williams.

"Height, weight, color of hair and eyes?" Buck rattled off the questions rapidly, only to be met with a vague look from his wealthy client.

"We have never been formally introduced, so I haven't seen him up close. I could say that he is very handsome, but I guess that doesn't help very much, does it?" Buck shook his head emphatically, recalling all the yo-yos and monkey-heads that women found attractive, and how there was no accounting for taste. He tapped his pencil absently. Addie screwed up her eyebrows with intense concentration. It was an expression she scrupulously avoided if she could, in deference to her smooth and as-yet-unlined forehead.

Buck cued her. "Hair?"

"Lots of it," Addie was able to report

enthusiastically. Then, realizing the answer he was waiting for, she added, "Brown." She thought some more. "He's quite tall, I'd say at least six-foot-two."

"Relationship?" Buck asked. Addie looked puzzled. Buck took it slow. "I mean, lady, the man is obviously a stranger to you. You say you've never even been introduced. You don't know the first thing about him. Neither do I. If you can clue me in, it could help me to help you."

Addie couldn't make sense of Buck's words. He smiled to encourage her. Then he continued. "Like—did he do something to you? Anything illegal or dangerous about him?"

She shook her head decisively. "For all I know, he's a perfectly legal young man. But he looks like a social climber. He's been trying to seduce, or has already seduced my daughter."

"*Her* name?" Buck interjected.

"Mrs. Scott Banning."

It was like pulling teeth, but Buck finally got enough down on paper to make a stab at investigating the suspect. In Buck's line of work, the world was divided into two groups: clients and suspects.

He shook Addie's hand as she got up to leave. Moments before, he had asked for the largest advance and day-to-day expense money of his career. The check was handed over without a quibble. The lady was truly a champ, and possibly a chump, but Buck considered her to be one helluva client.

She had almost reached the elevator when she remembered something and turned back to the office. When Buck looked up, Addie reached into her bag for an envelope and handed it to him. "A picture of my daughter," she said, by way of explanation. "It's another way of recognizing the man. Wherever you spot her, chances are he'll be somewhere close by."

The door closed behind her before Buck reached into the envelope and pulled out a picture of a very familiar face. So they were related—Julie Olson and Addie Olson— mother and daughter. Addie was not quite as young as she looked. He had noticed a little nip and tuck near the ear, almost hidden by the hairline. It was a good face-lift, but not good enough to fool a detective who kept up with the latest in skip-tracing and identity searches.

So Julie Olson turns up once again, he thought. *But this time, she's going to be the one spied upon.*

Buck briefly reviewed the notes he had taken, then leaned back, tipping the chair until his head rested against the wall. It was too late in the day to deposit the check, so he might as well relax, he concluded. Then he came upon one of the names he had scribbled—Mrs. Scott Banning. So Julie Olson had married! It hadn't been that long ago that he'd seen her, and she was single then. Some people might consider this to be still the honeymoon phase of the marriage. Julie Olson was obviously not among them.

According to her mother, she was already making out like crazy with this other guy.

He pulled out Julie's file once more. He checked the address and phone number in the telephone book. Still the same. Then he came upon the name Scott Banning. No wonder it sounded familiar. He was the guy who adopted the baby Julie wanted! That's what the whole court case was about! That's what he was hired for in the first place! At this rate, if Buck played his cards right and provided satisfactory service, he might expect another case from the same ever-widening circle of friends and relatives of Julie Olson Banning.

Buck pulled out his bottle of rye and took a healthy belt of it. When you're alone in the office, why bother with niceties like glasses and napkins? He wiped his mouth on his sleeve, shifted his bulk into a slightly tight raincoat, and left the belt dangling. A short visit to the local paper filled him in on Doug's connection with Knowlton Realty. Then on to a first-rate dinner with all the trimmings.

Addie rushed back to the hotel and checked in at the desk. The orders had arrived from Tiffany's and Cartier's on Fifth Avenue in New York City. Resplendently wrapped, they contained gifts for her first grandchild.

When she arrived at Julie's with an armful of presents, the baby's enthusiasm made up for Julie's lack of it. The strain between Addie and Julie had only increased with the years. Julie glanced at her watch and told her mother she was welcome to stay with little David as long as she liked, Carmen, the nurse, would be there through the evening. But Julie had some matters to attend to before meeting Scott for dinner.

At Addie's insistence, Julie reluctantly waited long enough to unwrap the sterling silver baby cup and utensils, and the other gifts. Her thanks to her mother were perfunctory. Then, a forced smile, and, "Gotta rush. 'Bye."

Addie longed to shout after her, "Don't keep Douglas waiting, dear," but managed to hold her tongue and resolved to bide her time. Before long, she'd have a report from Detective Harris which would probably confirm her most dire expectations.

Chapter Nine
A Friendship Begins

Buck Harris had a big decision to make. As was always the case with him, if it was something important, it had to do with money. The question was, how long should he string out his investigation of Doug Williams? He had more than enough right now to make any client sit up and take notice. It was difficult getting Williams' social security number, but once he had that, everything else fell into place. He had found the driver's license number, and from there the trail led upstate to the correctional facility where Williams had spent the past two years atoning for his questionable lifestyle.

It was a hefty file that sat on Buck's desk, waiting to be shared with Addie. But their understanding included a considerable *per diem* allowance, which would stop once he called her . . . It was almost worth a toss of a coin. But in the end, Buck's ego won out over his greed. He *had* to show the lady how swift and thorough he was, and hope that he would be rewarded with a suitable bonus.

Addie could concentrate on little else but the mysterious Doug Williams ever since she had first laid eyes on him. She kept reassuring herself that she was merely reestablishing her position of responsibility for her troubled daughter. There was no question in Addie's mind that Julie *had* to be troubled to marry Mr. White Bread and sneak around with Mr. Greek God. Addie herself had been unswervingly loyal to her late husband almost until the end—at least, that's what she told herself now. In the back of her mind she could remember a romantic attachment here and there when the going got especially rough with Ben. There was a certain way that his unbridled rage occasionally blazed out and incinerated anyone who stood in his way. At those times, Addie sought out other strong shoulders to lean on, other welcoming arms to comfort her.

But Julie was practically still on her honeymoon. The baby was still in diapers. This was a new marriage which needed a chance to grow. That was what Addie kept telling herself in a tone of self-righteous indignation. When Buck Harris called her, she was in his office, breathless, almost as soon as he hung up the phone.

Her curiosity was sated as her worst fears were confirmed.

"What can I tell you?" Buck shrugged.

"The guy's been a hustler and gambler since grade school. This was his only jail term. But on the other hand, it might have been the only time he got careless enough to get caught."

The photograph of Doug that Addie held in her hand hardly did the man justice. Perhaps the record didn't either. "What did you say he was doing now?" she asked.

"He's a salesman for Old Man Knowlton. You know, Knowlton Realty."

"But with his record, how did he get a job like that?" Addie asked.

"He was pretty slick there," Buck replied and he went on to explain how Doug had applied for the job. "It seemed like a great deal to everyone concerned. The old man didn't have to shell out a cent. Williams seems to be a great athlete and mixer, very popular at the country club and here in town. Dresses great, too. How he manages on the few tiny commissions he makes is really a puzzle . . ."

Buck let the last sentence dangle. He hoped that Addie would be as curious about that as he was. That would allow him to continue his investigation and pile up a few more days of work and added expenses.

"But if Mr. Knowlton knew he was an ex-convict . . ." Addie said, almost to herself.

"No reason to think he did. Chances are, this Williams character didn't even have to fill out an application for the job. You never do, if you're only working on commission," Buck replied.

Addie leaned back and opened her eyes wide in amazement as she thought of the implications of what she had learned. "Then, nobody knows."

Buck nodded. "Yeah. I guess that's how it is. Unless he went and told someone. But I can't see a smooth character like him going around and announcing that he was sent to the slammer and had to spend two years in stir."

Addie winced at the sound of the rude terms—*slammer, in stir*. There must be an entire vocabulary from which her lifestyle had sheltered her, she realized. Would her own daughter have to be exposed to it? She had to think carefully before taking the next step.

Once again, Buck suggested that there were a lot more juicy items and vital data to be pried out of the catacombs of the upstate judicial system. Just as it was illegal to use an unauthorized social security number to trace a person down, so there were other illegalities which Buck had mastered that enabled him to "cut through all the red tape"—or so he implied.

But Addie wasn't buying. She stood up and gave him her most gracious-lady smile as she extended her hand. "Mr. Harris, you have really impressed me with your outstanding work."

"So far," he said. "Wait till you see what I can come up with—"

Addie politely silenced him with a regal wave of the hand. "Let's wait a while on that, shall we?" she said in a quiet manner that invited no discussion. "You've given me an enormous amount of material to digest as it is." She glanced at the folder on his desk. "I can take that with me, can't I?"

Buck shrugged reluctantly and handed over the file. He wished he hadn't been so cheap about getting it professionally typed. He'd used a young niece who was taking typing in high school and was no better at spelling and punctuation than he was. Fortunately, he had made copies. "Sure," he said. "After all, you paid for it." Then he couldn't help adding, "Don't worry if you lose it or misplace it. I have copies." Buck knew that knowledge was power, and he didn't want Addie Olson to forget it.

For the rest of the day Addie wandered aimlessly, window-shopping for a while, and then stopping in a new cafe for drinks. Men flirted with her, but she didn't respond. She hardly noticed. She wondered what had gotten into her not to react to a civilized opening move from an attractive male. She worried about Buck Harris and hoped that the substantial bonus would keep him quiet—and keep him in her corner. She had hinted that she might need him in the indefinite future.

Now what? Addie pondered this for hours. One obvious choice was to march over to Julie's and slap the file down on her coffee table. Julie had been so uppity and disrespectful that Addie was tempted to do just that. But it would be too crude, she told herself, and she rejected the idea out of hand.

It might not be a bad idea to meet this fellow personally, Addie thought. A method immediately came to mind. As a woman of some financial substance, she might ask to be shown whatever real estate was on the market. But that presented a problem. If she called the agency, they might send her any one of the salespeople. She didn't dare ask for Doug by name. And if she asked Knowlton to send him, Doug might know in advance that he would be dealing with Julie's mother. He could either avoid meeting her altogether, or be put on his guard by Julie.

Addie's intention was to take Doug off-guard from the start. That way she could size him up. She was eaten up with curiosity as to what manner of man could so easily seduce her daughter.

The following morning at ten, Addie presented herself at Knowlton Realty. Old Man Knowlton was delighted to see her and sent out for coffee, eager to learn where Addie had been and what her plans for the future were. That led Addie into suggesting that she might be interested in settling down in Salem once again. Through the open door to the outer office she saw Doug at his corner desk. He had the phone in one hand and a pencil in the other.

Addie looked at Knowlton and pointed to Doug. Knowlton smiled, "Ah, Doug Williams. He's new in town, but we all have great hopes for his future in the real estate business."

Addie nodded. "Well, why don't you let *him* show me around? Maybe my purchase will help get him started." She had deliberately come in early enough to catch him before his afternoon interlude with Julie. Now she would have him cornered.

"Why not take my car?" Addie said to Doug, as he followed her outside with a catalogue of estates for sale under his arm. She led him to a long, sleek Mercedes, tossed him the keys, and said, "Here, you drive."

As Doug helped her into the passenger side and then slipped into the driver's seat, his sheer masculine presence and dazzling looks overwhelmed her. While he concentrated on adjusting to the unfamiliar gear shift and gauges, Addie concentrated on his classic profile and the strong hands on the wheel.

The name didn't connect at first. Mrs. Olson was almost as common as Mrs. Johnson or Jones or Brown. To Doug, Addie was just a glamorous, slightly older woman who seemed to have the dough to blow on a big sale for him.

To Addie, Doug was a younger, more vibrant, all-American version of Arne. He was quick, witty, and seemed very bright. For a fleeting second, Addie almost said to herself, *Ooohh, if only Julie hadn't found him first!*

But that was the point, wasn't it, she realized. Julie had found Doug—or Doug had sought out Julie. This stunning guy was a home-wrecker, Addie fumed. Or was he? She knew her daughter well enough to be convinced that Julie wasn't about to be led down anyone's garden path. The feeling, as the saying went, had to be mutual. And Addie had always felt that her daughter was more attractive than she. Indeed, there had been times during her marriage when she had felt that Ben paid more attention to Julie than to herself. When he came back from a long business trip, he always looked for his little daughter first, grabbing her and tossing her over his shoulder to make her giggle. *Then* he would embrace Addie.

But there was more to it than that. When Addie was a child, strong-willed and self-assured as she was about most things, she was uncertain about her looks. She grew up wearing glasses, which had long since been exchanged for contact lenses, of course. Her nose had been a trifle long and her chin a bit pointed. It had taken Ben's money and the best plastic surgeon in the business to create for Addie the image she had longed for in her youth.

It hadn't seemed fair that her daughter should grow up with flawless looks and not even be aware of how lucky she was. Addie had to work pretty hard for hers. Even now she watched every calorie while Julie gobbled up everything in sight and effortlessly maintained her slim figure.

As they drove away from one elephantine monstrosity of a house, they joked about it. "I just wanted you to see that one to get a sense of perspective," Doug said. "I think it must have started out as a Colonial until someone saw a rerun of *Gone With the Wind*."

Addie laughed. "There were enough columns on the front porch alone to hide the entire Confederate Army."

Her laugh reminded him of someone. Julie? He thought for a moment. Julie didn't laugh that often. And she certainly didn't have a sharp sense of humor, though it didn't seem to matter. She was so lovely in every other way that Doug didn't mind. It would have been nice if she could pick up one of his jokes and play with it or toss it back at him. But nobody could have everything. Julie had more than enough for Doug.

At the same time, Addie—she had insisted that he call her by her first name—was the most fun of any client he had dealt with at Knowlton's. With her constant stream of witty comments, he began to see each house, mansion, and estate with new eyes. *Boy*, he thought, *if I could remember just a few lines of her patter, I could give potential customers quite a charge.*

After a couple of hours of viewing homes, Addie called it quits for the day. "You've given me plenty to think about, Doug. Let me look over some of these pictures and descriptions. I'll get back to you real soon."

"Promise?" he asked her. For a moment Addie thought he was just using a smooth line, then he added sheepishly, "I could sure use a sale around now. Knowlton's going to get impatient with me real soon, and you know what? I don't know as I'd blame him."

That modest little confession evoked in Addie the tender feelings that no sophisticated line could ever produce. As she left him at the real estate office and drove away, she began humming to herself. She was utterly enchanted with him.

Halfway back to the hotel she remembered the purpose of her meeting with him. She knew that waiting on the desk beside her bed, back at the hotel, was a copy of Buck Harris's nasty file. In it were facts that she couldn't associate with Doug.

Now Addie was truly stymied. She could burn the file or mail it to Julie. She could advise her daughter or keep her lips sealed. Or she could have a drink and forget about it for a while.

The last choice seemed the most sensible.

Chapter Ten

An Affair Revealed

Things weren't working out quite the way Susan had planned. She felt that her logic was impeccable. The only problem was that the men she had counted on to be logical were turning out to be unpredictable.

Take the case of Doug Williams. The hip, savvy, hard-driven, and ambitious man came to town to romance rich women. Now that Susan had paid for the custom-tailored shirts, Bally shoes, British woolens and tweeds, and the rest of the wardrobe, to outfit him for his chosen role, he had gone soft on her. Twice he had tried to return her checks. Susan had merely mailed them back to him.

From the talk she heard at the hairdresser's, Doug was actually selling a few houses for his boss. She did a double-take when she heard this. It was almost beyond belief. She knew that he had taken the job just as an excuse to meet women. Then she realized what he must be doing—earning the money to pay her back.

Evidently, her plan to break up Julie's marriage to Scott was working better than she had dreamed it would. Julie had not only taken to Doug, but the two of them had fallen head-over-heels for each other. Nobody had told Susan this and the lovers were evidently being extremely discreet, for Susan had enough contacts to learn whatever was on the grapevine. No, in this instance, she put two and two together herself from the brief phone discussions she had had with Doug.

"What are you complaining about?" Susan demanded of him. "Haven't I paid you enough? Are you asking for more?" This exchange occurred on the occasion of Doug's first call on the subject.

"No. Quite the opposite. You've paid me much too much. I don't want to take a cent from you. In fact, I want to return everything you've given me already."

"What's the matter? Little Julie isn't good enough to seduce? Has she turned you off? Not your type?" By now, Susan was shouting.

"Calm down, will you?" Doug replied. "Julie Banning is one lovely lady. Any man would be proud to know her. No man needs to be *paid* to be nice to her."

"Ah ha!" Susan cooed maliciously. "You've fallen for her!" She had to admire him more for what he *didn't* say than for what he did.

First there was silence. Then Doug spoke in clipped, precise phrases. "Think what you like, lady. But remember what I'm telling you now. I want out!"

The sound of the receiver being slammed down with full force startled Susan and sent shivers down her spine. She wouldn't like to deal with Doug in person when he was in that mood. He might be violent.

She quickly dismissed her qualms about his temper. You can't have everything, she reasoned. She had what she wanted. There was no question in her mind now that Julie was having an affair with Doug. The next step was to try to get Scott to see it her way.

That turned out to be almost impossible. The Susan that Scott remembered had become hysterical when he'd broken the news to her that he was marrying Julie. She had ranted, screamed, and threatened to kill herself, but only *after* she had killed both of *them*. Thinking back to that occasion, Susan could begin to understand why Scott kept avoiding her and never returned her calls.

When a man owns his own company, it is easy for him to interpose personnel between himself and someone who wants to see him. Scott had a personal secretary who routinely screened all his calls. In this case, she was instructed to inform Susan Martin that he was out.

The house next door to Susan remained unoccupied. Scott had made no arrangements to sell it, but he and the baby had moved into Julie's expansive condominium in town. Calling him there meant going through Julie, and Susan wanted to avoid that as far as possible for the time being. Later, she would have plenty to say to Julie.

Once again, Susan tapped into the local grapevine. The owner of a construction company the size of Scott's couldn't stay hidden behind his desk forever. He had to be out in the field with his men. When Scott and Susan were living together, she knew each site he was working on. He even gave her a field number so that she could call him directly in case there was an emergency with the baby. Susan hoped and prayed that some day soon those old times would return. There might not be any way of taking the baby back from Julie, but once Scott found out how she was carrying on, Susan couldn't see him hanging around. Soon, the lights would be ablaze next door and everything would be as it was.

Next to the hairdresser's, the best source of local news was the town seamstress. Mrs. Malloy knew a good customer when she saw one, and Susan was among the best. Depending on her moods, Susan either lost all interest in food or binged. The more erratic her moods became, the more her waistline gained or lost inches. Right now, Mrs. Malloy was letting everything out and making a small fortune in the process.

By asking around, the seamstress was able to find a customer whose husband worked for Scott. The next time Susan dropped by with half-a-dozen skirts to be let out, Mrs. Malloy was able to give her a slip of paper listing the three construction sites Scott visited most frequently.

It was sort of like birdwatching, Susan told herself as she spent the quiet hours after dawn waiting at one or another of the sites with a pair of high-powered binoculars. There was no telling if Scott still had his old car or if he might go along with a group of workers in one of the company's trucks.

She finally spotted him several days later, just as she was giving up hope. He was wearing a bulky Irish-knit sweater and tweed cap. At a distance he was indistinguishable from his workmen, who also wore sweaters and caps. Up close, though, you could see that their caps were purchased at the ball park and their sweatshirts were worn and grimy. Still, she had to fine-tune the adjustments on her field glasses to pick him out of the crowd.

Susan felt a new rage boil within her. Julie had even changed Scott's image. When he was living with Susan, he'd pick out any old jacket and jeans to wear in the field. Now he could be Master of the Hounds at a British fox hunt.

She took a few minutes to pull herself together. If she came at him like a raging, out-of-control shrew, he could dismiss her without a second thought. She took the time to fix her makeup, run a comb through her hair, and breathe deeply a few times. Then she slowly got out of the car and approached him.

At first he didn't see her. Two of the men were unrolling a blueprint and pointing angrily to various sections, each accusing the other of making miscalculations in some sort of measurement. She waited on the sidelines, marveling at how masterfully Scott defused the argument. When they both nodded in agreement, Scott slapped each man on the shoulder and sent them back to work. He turned, and saw Susan staring him straight in the eye.

"Yes, it's me, Scott."

"And what in heaven's name are you doing out here?" he cried, alarmed and disturbed by her presence. "It isn't safe, you know. We're going to be blasting some of that rock over there pretty soon."

"I'm not afraid," Susan said.

"Well *I* am! You're not covered by our insurance. I'll ask you once to leave, and then I'll have to call the guard." He was, Susan could see, very rattled. But she was able to extract a promise from him to meet her a few minutes later if she left right away. "There's a diner just down the road," he said, more calmly. "Once we finish the blasting and I can leave someone in charge, I'll join you there."

At last they were seated together in the far corner of an almost deserted diner. Susan placed several photographs on the table in front of him. One showed Doug teeing off at the club, another had him swinging a tennis racquet, a couple more were shots of him simply walking, and two more were closeups.

Scott glanced quickly at them and said, "Looks vaguely familiar. Is he yours?"

"He looks *very* familiar to your *wife*, and he's *hers*," Susan snapped back.

Scott's fist shot out and banged the formica tabletop, scattering the pictures in all directions. Two remained on the table; the others fell to the floor.

"I wouldn't believe you even if you showed me compromising shots of Julie with the fellow, and you're too scattered and simple-minded to trick up a shot like that. These mean nothing. A few shots of a guy with a tennis racquet at the country club—"

"*Your* club, Scott. The one Julie has gone to since she was a kid. The place where she probably met him," Susan said in a trembling voice.

"Met who?" Scott retorted with disdain.

"His name is Doug Williams. He's new in town. He came here to meet attractive, rich women—and he's having an affair with Julie!"

Susan fairly shouted this last sentence as she lost control once again over her rising hysteria. The waitress kept mopping the counter, the cook kept stirring, and the only other customer was attempting dental surgery with a toothpick. Scott glanced around quickly and was relieved to see that no one had bothered to listen.

Then he grabbed Susan's wildly gesturing hands and pressed them palm-down on the table. When he had her attention he said very softly, "Susan, you are a very sick woman. I think you should get back to that psychiatrist of yours. What was her name again, was it Laura something-or-other?" As he spoke, he kept her hands on the table. He had realized that she wouldn't raise her voice if she couldn't gesture with her hands.

Susan bit her lips and began crying with frustration. "At least take the pictures with you. Or take a good look at them. You'll be seeing more and more of him in the vicinity of your wife. This way you can recognize him." The voice that moments before had harangued him, now pleaded with him.

Scott stood up. He scooped up the pictures on the table and, without looking at them, tore them up and placed the fragments neatly in the empty ashtray. Then he stepped over the others scattered on the floor and walked out. Susan put her head on the cold tabletop and cried hot tears.

When Scott got back to the site, he called his trusted lieutenants together. "Do you remember the woman who stopped me here earlier?" he asked. They nodded. "She is extremely emotionally disturbed. She sees things and hears things that no one else does. If you ever spot her here or on any of our sites, I want you to politely but firmly get her the hell away. It's less dangerous dealing with the explosives than getting within a mile of *her*."

Using the field phone, Scott relayed the same message to his personal secretary and told her to inform the others in the office. Throughout the rest of the day, his thoughts wandered back to Susan. He had immediately dismissed her accusations about Julie. They were not worth thinking about. He had been darned lucky to have chosen such a decent, loyal, wonderful wife. His head and heart left no room for doubts concerning his marriage.

Susan was something else again. He wondered how he could ever have been fool enough to consider her sane and emotionally stable. His thoughts went back to the months following Janet's death, when he was beside himself with grief. He wondered how he could actually have left his precious baby son in Susan's care while he went off to work every day. He could have hired someone, but Susan had insisted, had pleaded with him to let her take care of the baby. He shuddered to think what might have happened if she had gone off the deep end at that time.

By the end of the day, he had filed all these thoughts in the back of his mind. It would be unthinkable to bother Julie with them. He would not allow crazy Susan to become a source of concern to his beloved family.

Chapter Eleven

Taste of Revenge

Addie and Doug spent a few mornings tooling around in her sleek foreign car, looking at every expensive, extensive estate in the county. By this time Doug was receiving a living wage to supplement his commissions. When he told his boss that he wasn't sure that anything would pan out with Mrs. Olson, Old Man Knowlton told him not to concern himself about an actual sale. "She's a very important lady, a member of the international banking community. Having her as even a *potential* client can widen our contacts with her crowd. It certainly can't hurt, my boy."

With his boss's blessings and a stunning, witty woman for company, Doug felt like a king behind the wheel of a car he never dreamed he would have an opportunity to drive. When Doug was really happy, he expressed it by singing.

Addie was delighted. "Why, Doug, that's terrific! Sing another one," she'd implore, and he was glad to oblige. He never sang to Julie after the first time, when she'd wrinkled her brow and said, "Stop trying to sound like Frank Sinatra and pay attention to me." Julie liked rock-and-roll; anything from before Bob Dylan was old-fashioned to her.

Doug smiled and said to Addie, "I know some people who would say that my singing style is hopelessly out of date."

"That's only because melody has gone out of style, my dear," she said, urging him on to another song.

"What do you think of Bob Dylan?" he asked.

"A squeaky wheel," she said wryly. "If he got up on a bandstand, I'd have no urge to dance to what he calls music. I'd sit out the set with my hands over my ears. I guess I'm just an old-fashioned girl," she concluded, with an impish grin. "I like to be able to leave a dance floor still humming the melody."

This was music to Doug's ears. His musical idols were Frank Sinatra and Mel Tormé. He had practiced their style since he was a youngster dreaming of a singing career. Now his lovemaking with Julie always occurred to the background sounds of the Grateful Dead, the Jefferson Airplane, or the ever-present Mr. Dylan. It sometimes made him feel dated and sad that popular music was moving beyond him in this direction.

Addie boosted his ego as no woman had

for a long time. Part of him hoped that she would settle on a house soon so that he could rack up a big commission on the sale. But another part of him just wanted to spend happy mornings driving down tree-lined byways and country lanes, singing all the old favorites to an enthusiastic, attractive audience of one.

When Addie was not with Doug, she was thinking about him. The file which had been so thoroughly researched by Buck Harris now sat in the bottom of one of her suitcases, gathering dust. There was no question in her mind that whatever had happened in the past, he had turned over a new leaf and had rapidly grown into as solid a citizen as one could desire. And desire him she did, to the extent of trying to push images of Julie out of her mind.

One thought obsessed Addie. She could picture a scene in which Julie would ask Doug about his day and he would innocently mention this nice Mrs. Olson he was working with, trying to find her a house. As soon as Julie found out, she would see her mother's actions in the worst possible light. She might even be able to convince Doug that Addie had known who he was all along, and was playing him for a fool.

The odds against Addie narrowed each day she spent with him. How much longer could he see the mother in the morning and the daughter in the afternoon and not make some sort of connection? A chance remark, a stranger's question—"How's the family?"—

and everything would be destroyed.

Addie waited until she felt that there was a genuine bond between them before she mentioned the connection herself. She brought it up as innocently as she could. "I'm not really sure that I should move back to town permanently, Doug," she said one day when they stopped for mid-morning coffee. "I know it's a little late in the game to say such a thing. I mean, you've spent so much time with me."

Doug immediately assured her that it was a pleasure spending time with her, and that his boss had no complaints about his schedule. "Is something wrong?" he asked, with genuine concern.

"I've just been having some second thoughts," she said. "Some *sad* second thoughts." She paused and assumed her most vulnerable expression. It was the one that brought strong men rushing to her side.

Doug coaxed her further. "Look, Addie, I think we know each other pretty well by now. I'd be flattered if you'd consider me a friend, someone you can lean on."

"It's my daughter," Addie said. "In recent years we haven't been getting along as well as we should. There's been a strain. She blames me for some of the problems she had with her father, my late husband."

"Is she away at school?" he asked. He pictured a young child or perhaps someone just entering adolescence.

"No such luck. She's married, with a baby." When she saw the look of puzzlement on his face she realized that he was re-estimating her age, adding on another decade or so. She wanted to say jokingly, "She's a child bride, of course"—it wasn't that far from the truth. Instead, she kept silent and gave him room to think.

"She must be awfully young," Doug said.

Addie nodded. "That she is."

"Where does she live?" he asked.

"Right here in Salem. *That's* the problem, you see. If there's any strain in our relationship, perhaps I should rethink my priorities. It might be better for all concerned if we weren't in the same town."

"Surely Salem is a big enough place for both you and Mrs. . . ." He paused, then asked, "What *is* her name."

"Julie," Addie said sweetly, trying to hide her nervousness. "Mrs. Scott Banning. You might have run into her at the club."

It was then that Addie really took the measure of the man. Doug kept the same expression and became preoccupied with stirring his coffee. Addie could picture the wheels going around in his head as he connected mother to daughter.

"She plays a pretty good game of tennis," Addie said, to cover the silence. Her tone was helpful, as if she were trying to help him picture who this Julie Banning could be. Doug kept stirring until Addie was sure that he'd wear out either the spoon or the cup. Finally, when she could stand the silence no longer, he made an exaggerated gesture of looking at his watch.

145

"Yes, it *is* getting late," Addie agreed emphatically. "I almost forgot, I have an appointment at the bank, and I'd like to get there before lunch. Will you forgive me?"

The gratitude shone in Doug's eyes. She could tell that he had a great deal of thinking to do before he could feel at ease with her again. The less she said right now, the better.

When Doug dropped himself off at the real estate agency and handed her the car keys, Addie felt almost too exhausted to drive back to the hotel. They smiled vacantly and waved to each other. Something was said about Addie taking a few days off to think through her "family problem." The brief conversation over coffee had drained both of them.

Addie had lunch sent up to her room together with a pitcher of martinis. The luncheon was for one. The pitcher could float a party. An hour later, she fell into a restless, dream-filled sleep.

Susan looked entirely different as she sat opposite Julie Banning at Doubles, the smart new private club for dining and dancing that had opened up in Salem just a few months earlier. It stated firmly, "Membership by invitation only." Scott found the policy a little pretentious and snobbish, but he had to agree with his wife that the food and service were first-rate. When they planned to meet there around dinnertime and Scott was unexpectedly delayed, the policy of the club ensured that his wife could wait for him alone without being flirted with, hurried, or harassed.

Today was the exception. Once again, Susan's seamstress had come in handy. She was able to put Susan in touch with a son-in-law who worked in the kitchen at Doubles. With his help, she gained access to the dining room. Remembering from their years of friendship that Julie would do anything to prevent a scene, she crossed the dining room to the alcove where Julie was seated alone, sipping a long, cool drink.

Susan had spent half the day making herself presentable. After returning from her disastrous meeting with Scott, she took one look in the mirror and cried at the sight of her wild, frizzy blond hair shooting out in all directions, her plaid jacket and jeans and field glasses. She resolved to look as sophisticated as possible from then on. She hadn't entirely succeeded this time, but at a casual glance, the headwaiter and bartender saw nothing amiss.

Julie, by contrast, had spent another dazzling afternoon of lovemaking with Doug. He had been as masterful and considerate and sexy as always. She had gone home to shower and change, looked in on the baby, and then stopped by the new dining club for a drink. For weeks now, she had been considering herself the luckiest woman in the world. She had a kind, considerate, sincere husband, a beautiful baby, and a lover that women dream of but never seem to find.

She let out an inadvertent gasp when

Susan slid into the seat opposite her. Since she was alone in that section of the room, off in an alcove, and the waiters were preoccupied elsewhere, nobody noticed.

"I'm only going to take five minutes of your time," Susan said. "It's about Doug."

That magic name captured all of Julie's attention. She looked stricken for a moment. Her first thoughts were that Susan had spotted the two of them together and was about to blackmail her. Or worse still; for since Susan did not want for money, she could not be bribed. She might simply run to Scott and tell him everything. Julie wished she had it in her power to banish Susan forever from the face of the earth, for she was content with life. Two men in love with her and a baby boy who cried for her—that was Julie's idea of heaven.

Now the serpent herself sat down at the table: Susan—the wild-haired killer of Julie's first and truest love, a woman capable of anything. Julie wanted to scream. But the part of her brain that computed what was practical warned her to remain silent and poised. She was a grown woman now. One way or another she could keep a lid on things—if she didn't lose control.

"I just want five minutes of your time," Susan continued, "to tell you about Doug Williams." Julie looked bewildered. What would Susan want to tell *her*? She sat back, pulled the cherry out of her drink and bit it off the stem, trying to hide her nervousness.

Susan reached into her handbag, opened

her wallet and pulled out a canceled check. "Doug Williams was paid by me to seduce you." Julie looked stunned. Susan rephrased her statement. "To make love to you, Julie. I *paid* him. See—here's a check."

Julie said weakly, "It could have been for anything. What does a check prove?" But her voice lacked conviction.

Once again Susan reached into her purse. This time she pulled out a series of department store bills from Blessington's. "Remember the tweed jacket with the suede patches? The Bally shoes? The London Fog raincoat? The tennis racquet? The set of championship golf clubs?"

As Susan ran down the list of items, she laid down the bills and receipts one after another, like someone throwing down a winning hand of bridge. All the blood seemed to drain from Julie's face. She was chalk white. Her large eyes stared in shock as if from a ghostly mask. She stood up without saying a word, picked up her bag, and began walking toward the exit. Susan gathered together all the papers quickly and shouted after her.

"He's bought and paid for, Julie, bought and paid for!"

The headwaiter rushed in to see what was the matter. He looked questioningly at Julie, who signaled him to get rid of Susan. As Julie stood outside waiting for her car to be driven around, she saw two of the kitchen help strongarm Susan out the back door. Julie got into her car and sped away with

Susan's voice still ringing in her ears: "Bought and paid for, he's bought and paid for!"

When she arrived home, she called Scott's office and was able to reach him just as he was heading out the door. "Sorry, honey, but it was the same old story. Another stupid emergency. Are you calling from the restaurant?"

"No, from home. I've got this terrible headache and sore throat. I think I'm coming down with something."

"Oh, my poor baby," Scott said, his voice filled with concern. "I'll head straight home. You get right into bed. Is there anything I can get for you?"

By the time Scott arrived, Julie was under the covers pretending to be asleep. She didn't trust her emotions and wanted to avoid all the men in her life for a while until she got her head and heart together.

Carmen stayed with little David and Scott watched television. To the sound of a ballgame and a baby's occasional cries, Julie reviewed the last few months and did some good hard thinking.

Scott refused to go to work the next morning until he was able to look at Julie and see for himself how she was feeling. The drawn face and the red, puffy eyes with deep shadows beneath them translated easily into a bad case of the flu.

"No, Scott, I really feel much better," Julie protested. "It must have been just a bug I picked up, a sort of twenty-four-hour virus."

She was preparing for the possibility that she might want to go out later in the day. "Don't get too close to me," she cautioned, "I don't want to you catch it."

Now that Susan knew about her affair, all the romance had gone out of it. Now that Julie believed that Doug had been bribed to make love to her, everything seemed sordid. She could hardly stand to face Scott at all until it was resolved. She forced herself to eat a piece of toast and part of an egg. Food was the last thing on her mind, but she knew she would need her strength for what lay ahead.

Up until now, she had been careful never to call Doug at the office. It made no sense to break that rule at this late date. She would soon be seeing him at their normal meeting place. This suited Julie's purpose well enough. Forewarned is forearmed. Julie wanted Doug to have no hint that, rather than a romantic meeting, this was to be a final confrontation. She wanted to see the look on his face.

Chapter Twelve
A Sudden Marriage

It was a mystery to Doug why a strained-looking Julie should push him away and suggest that they just drive. It was the first time that she had rejected his embrace. But he made no protest and, following her clipped instructions, drove along aimlessly with no direction in mind. When they had passed Lookout Point, he pulled up to a group of benches and empty picnic tables. Julie remained silent as he turned off the engine. Finally he got out, walked around to her side of the car, and opened the door for her. "If you have something on your mind, here's as good a place to spill it as any," he said.

Julie nodded without expression and followed his long easy strides to a rustic wooden table. He seated himself on a bench. She walked around the table and seated herself opposite him. *This is going to be something really heavy,* Doug thought. There was plenty to choose from. It might be his prison record, his friendship with Addie, his . . .

"I saw Susan Martin yesterday," Julie began. Doug nodded. He looked shocked. "I see you know what I'm about to say," Julie continued.

Julie's voice had never sounded so metallic to Doug before. Her words had never sounded so clipped. He was listening to a woman who seemed like a stranger.

"I looked up *gigolo* in the dictionary," she continued. "It's a man who is paid to be a woman's lover and is supported by her—"

"No!" Doug shouted. Julie turned aside. "Listen to me! You've got it all wrong!"

She continued as if there had been no interruption. "Your case is something special. One woman paid you to make love to another woman." Doug's eyes pleaded with her for understanding. Instead, her steely voice took on a sarcastic tone as she said, "Now that should be one for the *Guinness Book of World Records.*"

"For God's sake," Doug yelled, "will you let me get a word in edgewise?"

"Sure," Julie said wryly, "be my guest. But before you begin lying, let me warn you that Susan showed me the canceled checks and all the bills for your clothes and sporting equipment."

Nothing Doug said was able to make a dent in Julie's conviction. She was the hanging judge and he was the condemned prisoner. He talked, she sneered. It escalated to a shouting contest. Everything ended at the rear entrance of Blessington's just as it had in happier days. This time neither of them doubted the finality of the curt, harsh goodbye.

But Doug made one last stab at explaining things. He got together all of the letters with checks enclosed he had sent to Susan to pay her back for the money she'd advanced to him. Each of them had been returned unopened. Now he sent the batch to Julie, marked *personal,* care of the country club. That way she'd be sure to see it without her husband opening it by mistake. The entire envelope came back unopened.

Doug realized that he had been under a strain ever since he'd found out that Addie was Julie's mother, and that he was the common thread between two warring factions. With Julie breaking off the relationship for an entirely different reason, he felt himself sliding into a depression. He dropped a note off to his boss saying that he needed a few days to take care of some personal matters.

For three days the most active aspect of Doug was his beard, which grew at a prodigious rate while his razor sat on the shelf. A bout with a bottle didn't last very long. Doug had too many unhappy childhood memories of drunken men visiting his mother and beating him up whenever they thought he was in the way. If that was what too much booze did to people, he didn't want *that* kind of habit further complicating his already unbearable life.

Food was another matter. When he drank, he lost his appetite. When he stopped drinking, his feeling for food didn't come back. By the time Addie got to him, he looked like a gaunt, stubble-faced prisoner of war.

It had taken only a couple of days of enforced absence for Addie to feel an intense longing for Doug. When she put on her perkiest voice and called him at the realtor's, she was devastated to find that he would be out for a few days.

She tracked him down to his rooming house, wondering what had gone wrong and where she might fit into the mystery. As soon as she saw the two bloodshot eyes peering out of the long, sad face, she threw caution to the winds, brushing past him into his room.

The room was a mess. Catalogues, real estate files, and clothes overflowed the one chair. The narrow bed was a jumbled mess of sheets. Doug gestured helplessly and said, "I'd ask you to sit down, but . . ."

He shrugged and collapsed onto the bed. Addie sat down beside him. "Oh, my poor Doug. What's happened? Who or what could have put you into such a state?"

"I broke up with my girl," he said.

In the silence that followed, Addie realized that she was safely out of the breakup. Otherwise, he would have said "your daughter" instead of "my girl."

In a still, small voice Addie said, "I love you, Doug. I don't know if that helps in any way, but it's true. I *do* love you. I've realized it for a while, but I didn't dare to say anything before now."

"You picked yourself a loser, lady," he responded. "I'm not much good to anybody. Just a loser, all the way down the line . . ."

"I have *never* picked a loser, as you well know," Addie said firmly. "I can spot one a mile off. I promise you two things, Doug. First, you are *not* a loser. Second, I'd bet my life on you. I *want* to bet my life on you."

"What are you talking about, Addie?"

"I want to marry you."

Again there was silence. Then Doug said, "You won't, after I tell you a couple of things about myself."

Here it comes, Addie thought. "I *will,* in spite of what you tell me as long as you'll love in me return."

Again there was silence. Addie tried to concentrate on the cracks in the paint that ran up the wall and across the ceiling. This was the time for her to hold her tongue.

Doug thought back over the short, happy period that he had known Addie. Her jokes had tickled him. She had encouraged him in his work and in his singing. He had a crazy vision of the two of them someday singing together in the shower. Then he abruptly changed his train of thought. His voice grew tense. "I have to trust your discretion in order to tell you this first thing. I have been going with a married woman. We've been seeing each other behind her husband's back."

"Say no more," Addie said. "As long as it's over, let's leave the poor woman her privacy. You don't have to tell me who it is." Addie was actually afraid she would not be able to look sufficiently surprised once she heard Julie's name.

Doug nodded, pleased that *that* was out of the way. The second thing was even harder. "My past," he said. "I've been in prison."

"How many times?" Addie asked, knowing the answer.

"Once."

"Everybody makes mistakes," Addie said. "You, at least, can say you paid for yours."

"It was for some fancy bookkeeping. You know, illegalities to save my boss money. He was going through a divorce and his wife was his business partner. He wanted to show smaller profits so she'd claim less money from him."

Addie nodded. His account tallied with Buck Harris's right down the line.

"Later, after he showed me how, I did the same number on him. I shouldn't have, but I used to gamble and I ran up a lot of debts."

"Do you gamble anymore?"

He shook his head.

"Would you gamble on *me?*" Addie asked.

Doug couldn't believe what he was hearing. "After all that?"

Addie smiled. "I like to be practical. We've spent so much of Old Man Knowlton's time looking at all those fancy old houses. The least I can do is pick one to live in. I don't want to ramble around a huge old place all alone. We share similar tastes, so . . ."

Her humor finally got through to Doug. When she hugged him, he returned the hug and kissed her gently, then sensuously.

"If I get us a piano and brush up on my sight-reading, will you sing some the the old songs I play?"

That clinched it. Addie hung around while Doug shaved and showered. She didn't want to let him out of her sight for a moment, lest he change his mind. When he had finally pulled himself together and looked presentable, they climbed into her car and drove upstate. They wanted to get to another county before looking for a justice of the peace. Before the afternoon ended, they were pronounced man and wife.

Chapter Thirteen

A Death in the Family

Old Man Knowlton joked that Doug was the second employee of his who'd wound up as a customer. But unlike Susan, who had bought a home on a whim and fallen in love with her next-door neighbor, Mr. and Mrs. Douglas Williams proceeded carefully, involving their banker and a staff of attorneys in the completion of the purchase.

Addie had known just what she wanted all along. Now she had the perfect house and a handsome husband to go with it.

Bermuda had been the ideal choice for a honeymoon. Addie reasoned that it was romantic enough to dazzle Doug on his first trip out of the United States; at the same time, everyone spoke English. Even after years abroad with her late husband, Addie still hadn't mastered any other language.

Doug was delighted to discover that Addie looked as good in a bikini as any other woman on the beach. She was no match for him on the tennis court—no woman was. But they acquitted themselves at mixed doubles. Above all, they loved sailing. Doug surprised Addie with his proficiency at the tiller of a forty-foot boat. They had the hotel prepare a sumptuous box lunch and fill a wine cooler with champagne. Doug discovered all sorts of isolated coves where they could put down anchor, sunbathe, and make love.

It was there that Doug told her stories about his miserable childhood, and his struggles along the road that led to his one term of imprisonment. Addie demonstrated the sort of sympathy and understanding that he never dreamed he could evoke—let alone deserve—from a woman.

One day, while Doug was downstairs making arrangements for the rental of a sailboat, Addie used the opportunity to call home. When Alice answered, Addie told her mother about the marriage and carefully spelled out Doug's full name. "Neither of us wanted to bother with an announcement in the paper before we left," she explained casually, "but I did want the family to know."

"Have you told your daughter yet?" Alice asked.

"No, Mother, I thought that I'd leave it up to you," Addie answered, trying to keep her voice on an even keel.

"Well, if he's as wonderful as you say he is," Alice responded, "I'm sure Julie will be crazy about him, too."

That was what Addie was afraid of. If she had merely wanted to inform her family, she could have easily waited until they returned. Remembering Julie's temper, which could be almost as awesome as her late father's, Addie wanted to give her daughter enough breathing room to absorb the news while she and Doug were out of the country.

The second call Addie made was to her bankers. She instructed them to assign one officer to create a bank box number for all her financial mail, stock issues, bond statements, and other fiscal matters. That way, she could consult her banker about money decisions whenever she cared to while keeping it out of her home. She loved Doug and trusted him—up to a point. If his weakness had been "creative accounting" in the past, such things might have a tendency to recur, like certain strains of tropical hepatitis. Far better to keep temptation out of the way.

Scott Banning was concerned about his wife. Her virus, or whatever it was, seemed to have put her in a blue funk. She either snapped at him or didn't talk at all. She paid almost no attention to the baby. She seemed restless most of the time. The exception was when they dimmed the lights before going to sleep. Then she had a headache which precluded making love. Something was going on, but he was damned if he could figure out what it was. He decided to give her another few days and then insist that she see her grandfather for a general check up. As for Julie herself, too much was going on for her to contain within herself, and there was no trusted friend with whom to share it.

Fortunately, her grandmother couldn't see the look on her face when she learned about Doug and Addie. "Why, what's the matter, dear?" Alice had asked when she heard Julie gasp on the other end of the phone line. "Have you heard of him? Is there something wrong?"

Julie was able to avoid the questions and cut the conversation short by telling her grandmother that the baby was crying. The child was actually playing happily with his nurse, Carmen, but when he heard his mother hang up the phone and then give out a long, keening wail, he joined in. Carmen looked helplessly from mother to son. Finally Julie shouted at her to take the baby out to the park so that she could cry in peace.

Julie had a week and a half to plan her next move. This sudden marriage was crazy. She was certain that Doug didn't love her mother. She was almost certain that he couldn't even know Addie very well. How had they met? When? Where? There were so many questions that had to be answered. She needed to talk face to face with either or both of them. Until she knew where she stood and what could be salvaged, she was in no mood to discuss any of it with Scott.

When she finally did get together with her mother and Doug, it was over lunch at the country club. The two honeymooners were attractively tanned and looked exceptionally fit and in love. Julie looked drawn and haunted.

"Well, aren't you going to congratulate us and wish us well?" asked Addie. Her innocent tone had been perfected on those occasions over many years when she'd needed to pull the wool over her late husband's eyes. Julie would have recognized it if she weren't so outraged at the sight of the two of them together.

Before Julie could answer, however, Addie was paged to the phone. She waved merrily at the two of them, promising to be right back. "You did this to spite me," Julie spat out. "You can still get out of it, you know."

Doug shook his head. "I don't want to," he said.

"You don't love her, you love her money. Why bother with the daughter when Mom's got all the dough!"

Again Doug shook his head and said, "You're wrong, Julie."

"How long will you be happy with a grandmother?" Julie taunted.

"As long as she's happy with me," Doug answered quietly.

"What's that I hear?" Addie said brightly, returning to the table. She turned to Doug and said, "That was the bank, dear. The closing on the house is set for Tuesday."

Julie pointed to Doug and snapped at Addie, "How much do you know about him?"

"As much as I need to know to love him." Addie beamed a loving smile at Doug.

"Did you know that Doug and I were having a long affair and you probably picked him up on the rebound?"

"If that's the case," Addie said amiably, "how lucky for all of us that it turned out as well as it did. Now let's order lunch, shall we? I'm getting awfully hungry."

Julie stood up and walked away without another word. Addie sat there calmly examining the menu. Doug waited tensely, with a lump in his throat, wondering what she was going to say. In the distance they heard the sound of squealing tires and a honking horn as Julie sped away like a bat out of hell.

"I think the red snapper sounds nice, dear. That and a green salad. How about you?" She put the menu down and looked Doug in the eye.

"I tried to tell you—" he began.

"I remember, Doug. The married lady you had just broken up with. I was the one who stopped you from naming her. And you know what?"

Doug shook his head, looking miserable.

"It was probably just as well. Who needed family complications to get in the way of true love? And it is true love, isn't it?"

Doug leaned over and kissed Addie.

"One thing I never asked you," Addie said. "What on earth led you here to Salem in the first place?"

Doug reminded her about how he and Bill

Horton had formed a close friendship. It had come out, on one of those lingering tropical evenings, that he and Bill had been cellmates. "In a way, then," Addie had mused, "it was meant to be, wasn't it?" The Susan Martin part of the story he edited slightly. At this stage, he thought, it would simply be stupid to bring her into the picture. "And so, after all the nice things Bill said about this place, when I passed it on the way down county I thought I'd give it a try."

Addie thought for a minute. "You know, my mother tells me that Bill will be getting out pretty soon. Why don't we both take a trip upstate to that prison and visit him, as sort of a pre-homecoming?"

Doug knew exactly what Addie was thinking and readily agreed. Far better to smooth things over with Bill beforehand and get his blessing. Everyone in the family might not be as understanding as Addie about Doug's background. Now that he had paid his debt to society, there really wasn't any good reason why they had to know. It was up to Bill.

Several days later, Addie and Doug drove up to visit Bill Horton. Anything Addie knew about prisons and ex-cons she had learned from mysteries and television shows. She seemed to recall something about ex-offenders being instructed not to mix with other criminals. "Is there anything wrong with your going in there with me?" she asked.

Doug shook his head. "I served out my complete sentence. Now I can do almost anything I please. If I were on probation, it would be another matter. But I'm free as a bird. Maybe that's the trouble," he said, referring to the butterflies in his stomach. Once he had been released from prison, he had vowed never to lay eyes on the place again. In addition, he didn't want to announce his new life and lifestyle to old cronies, lest they attempt blackmail later, or something equally unsavory.

Once again they were lucky. Because of Bill's background, good behavior, and imminent release, he was allowed an afternoon pass. Doug waited at the hotel in the next town while Addie went to the prison gates to pick Bill up.

Bill Horton spent the first few moments in Addie's company rejoicing at seeing his sister. They had been separated not only by his prison stint, but by her lengthy stay in Europe, and had a great deal to catch up on. But first, she announced her marriage to Doug.

Bill took it in his stride. Though he recalled Doug's future plans included finding himself a female meal ticket, one look at the happiness and contentment that shone in his sister's eyes and he bowed to the inevitable. He remembered his late brother-in-law only too well; Doug was bound to be an improvement, if indeed he had truly reformed.

It was easy enough for Bill's old friendship

with Doug to resume once he and Addie arrived at the hotel. By silent agreement, they kept their conversation away from what was going on among mutual acquaintances behind bars. They had a long leisurely lunch while Bill was brought up to date on hometown activities. "It seems so strange having my old jailhouse buddy fill me in on family and friends," Bill marveled.

"Well, it was all those kind words you had about Salem that made Doug homesick for a place he had never even seen," Addie said, smiling at the two of them.

"Has it lived up to your expectations?" Bill asked Doug.

Doug nodded enthusiastically. "You bet. I'm crazy about it." He and Addie told Bill all about their new home. "You can be one of our first guests," Doug added, "that is, until you've gotten yourself settled and back at work."

Bill's face fell. "What's wrong, Bill?" Addie asked. "Don't you plan to return to Salem and continue your practice at the hospital?"

"It's not what I want to do that counts," he replied sadly. "Don't forget, I'll be an ex-con. Not only that, since they're letting me out early, I'll be on parole. That means I'll have to report regularly to a parole officer. Can you picture the State Medical Board or the board of directors of Salem General Hospital allowing me to practice under those conditions?"

Addie and Doug cheered him up the best they could, and Addie promised to use whatever influence she had, reminding Bill that his own father was pretty powerful in the medical community.

After they left Bill at the gate, they began the drive home, picturing the handsome surgeon returning to his cell to count the days until his release. Then Addie had a thought. Turning to Doug she said, "After all this talk about Bill's plans, I realize that we've never really discussed yours. I'll love you just as much if you do anything or nothing, but I am curious about it."

"It won't be nothing, that's for sure," said Doug. "I intend to earn a respectable living to the full extent of my abilities." Then he added, "Whatever they may be."

Addie began to worry, remembering his past problems. "It won't be with accounting or bookkeeping, will it?"

Doug shook his head. "Don't worry, I've had it with numbers. All they added up to was two years in jail. That part of my life is over." As they drove in silence, Doug fiddled with the radio, finding nothing but rock-and-roll or country-and-western. He turned it off in disgust.

"Who needs a radio when I have my favorite singer seated beside me?" Addie said. "How about it? Let's hear a few of the oldies but goodies . . . the ones on the top of *my* hit parade."

Doug sang the rest of the way home. His spirits rose, and he breathed easier, feeling that he had been through the worst the fates could toss at him, and survived. His wife loved his voice and he loved to sing. All began to look right with the world.

For Julie Banning, life seemed to hold nothing but bitterness and regret. The baby she had fought so hard for had grown irritable and had begun crying more than usual. Carmen had tried to explain that the little boy was only echoing Julie's mood, but she was afraid to be too explicit, lest she be considered out of place. But however broad the hints, Julie was incapable of picking up on them.

Scott was on one of his quarterly trips out of town inspecting new tractors and earth-moving equipment. Without him to answer to, Julie just sat around and brooded, leaving the day-to-day planning to Carmen and the daily help.

She knew that she could not go on this way indefinitely. She had to take a decisive step in one direction or another. Once Scott returned and took a look at the state that she and the house were in, he would do what he had been threatening: He would contact her grandfather either to give her a checkup himself, or send her to someone else. She was concerned that the someone else might be a psychiatrist . . . like maybe her Aunt Laura.

Enraged at the very idea of it, Julie decided that no one would have that power over her. That included her husband. Now that Doug had deserted her, life with Scott held no meaning.

171

Julie recalled the endless discussions among the women at the club regarding the best hairdressers, plastic surgeons, and divorce lawyers. She looked through the local phone directory under "Lawyers" until she found the name that most of the women mentioned favorably. She made an appointment for the next morning.

When Scott returned that evening, Julie had straightened up the rooms and made herself presentable. Scott read signs of improvement in her appearance and her civil greeting, even though she was still cold and distant. He loved her so much that he read favorable signs wherever he could.

Julie was still asleep when he left for work the next day. Actually, she was merely pretending. As soon as the door closed behind him, she showered, dressed, and left for her appointment with the lawyers. Two hours later, she returned home, having set the machinery in process to file the preliminary papers leading to a divorce.

After spending so many days at home and then finally taking such an action, Julie felt drained. She was napping when the call came from Scott's office—her husband had been crushed by a wrecking ball which had fallen from a crane at one of the building sites. He was being rushed to the hospital.

Tom Horton met Julie at the hospital desk on the main floor, just inside the double doors. From the look on her grandfather's face, she knew to prepare herself for the worst.

Scott had regained consciousness, before Julie arrived, just long enough to see Tom Horton leaning over him. "Tell Julie I've always loved her and I always will," he whispered. As Tom explained, there was really nothing the hospital could do. It was a miracle that he lasted the short time that he did.

"Don't let yourself fall apart," Tom said. "We'll all stand by you and give you all the support you need. But don't forget that little David needs you now more than ever."

Chapter Fourteen

New Lives

Bill Horton was clearing the last few items out of his cell—he would be leaving in only a few more hours—when a letter arrived from his mother. It concerned Laura. "Aren't we all lucky that they put Mickey's wife in charge of the character committee?" he read. "Mickey is going to help her all he can in getting witnesses together who will shout from the rooftops to the whole world what a fine gentleman you are."

Bill smiled at how far his mother seemed to be from the truth, and wondered if every criminal's mother was as prejudiced in her son's favor. *Criminal* was the correct word, he felt, even though he had always considered that he was serving time for the wrong offense.

In Bill's mind, his crime had been against Laura. He had confessed it in a letter to her so that she could use it against him—he hoped, as a kind of atonement, to put the means of his punishment quite literally in her hands. But fate came out of left field and dealt him an unexpected blow. His brother Tommy's malicious wife, Kitty, had accosted him in the middle of a busy hospital corridor and threatened to tell the world that he'd fathered Laura's baby. The way she'd put it made Laura seem like a slut, a woman who slept around.

Bill could take any slander the vengeful woman could sling at him, but he couldn't allow Laura and Mickey to be smeared by the same hurtful tattle.

His only thought had been to calm Kitty down so that he could reason quietly with her. When she continued to spew forth the gossip, he reached out to shake her by the shoulders.

Her death was finally determined to have resulted from that shaking. Once it had been established in court that Bill had no knowledge of Kitty's longstanding heart condition, he was sentenced for involuntary manslaughter.

Bill's term was as short as an understanding judge could in good conscience allow. Once it became only a matter of weeks before his release, he'd spent almost every waking moment thinking about the woman he still loved and the baby he could never claim.

Doug and Addie drove upstate on the day that Bill was released. They insisted that he stay with them. He agreed to stay for the first few days. "You'll be our very first guest," Addie announced. "We haven't even finished fixing the house up."

"It's still a cut above Upstate Pen, and I'm a guy who knows what he's talking about," Doug said.

"I hope Mom isn't planning one of her big homecoming feasts," Bill observed. "I have too many other things to worry about first."

Laura was taking care of those worries one at a time. She had assembled an impressive group for the character committee to question. Bill's fame as a practicing surgeon at the Upstate Medical Center had spread, for he had originated surgical innovations and perfected new techniques which were still being successfully used. In addition, as an unpaid volunteer physician for the Red Cross in California, he'd helped hundreds of grateful GIs, who wrote letters in his behalf.

"All of this is very well and good," Dr. Sternwood grumbled in a tone of voice that belied his words. "Let's even say, for the sake of argument, that Bill Horton was a virtual saint until the day that woman was shaken to death. I'd still like that action to be addressed by you, Dr. Spencer, before we proceed any further toward Bill Horton's absolution and beatification."

Sternwood was new in town, and new to the hospital, with a doctorate in hospital administration, not medicine. His cutting words and officious attitude were rapidly gaining him the reputation for sarcasm far beyond the call of duty. Though Laura had never been called upon to deal with him directly before, she had heard all about his tactics.

Now she knew what she had to do. When Tommy Horton first offered to help his brother in any way that he could, Laura concluded that he had been through more than enough already. After years as a prisoner of war in Korea, he had first had to submit to extensive, painful corrective surgery and then suffer the sudden, unexpected death of his wife. Laura had almost lost track of Tommy. He didn't visit the family much. He went to work, and spent the evenings alone, taking care of his little girl. Laura explained it to herself as Tommy's way of adjusting to culture shock as well as the loss of a wife.

When Laura called, Tommy was waiting by the phone. He arrived at the top floor conference room looking trim, neatly dressed, and painfully shy. The honesty shone from his eyes as he spoke and the board was quite moved by what he had to say.

"I know very little about medicine, considering the number of doctors in the family," he said quietly. "But I can assure you that no member of the family, and that includes me, knew that there was anything wrong with Kitty's heart. Laura has probably told you that Kitty's own doctor warned her for years about her condition and gave her regular prescriptions and pills to take in an emergency. If she took those pills, it was behind locked doors or when no one else was around.

"As you might tell from what I'm saying, my wife was in many ways a difficult woman. She was the kind you sometimes wanted to grab and shake some sense into."

There was complete silence as everyone in the room thought long and hard about Tommy's last sentence.

"When she screamed, you wanted to quiet her," he went on. "When she got very agitated, you wanted to calm her down. But when she screamed or got agitated, she was incapable of hearing anything anyone said. She kept screaming." He paused and swallowed. "She did this until you wanted to shake her just to hear yourself think."

Again there was silence throughout the room. Laura didn't dare look at Sternwood to see how he was taking it, but his silence alone was a good sign.

Tommy picked up a glass and filled it from the pitcher on the conference table. Laura whispered, "Take it easy, Tommy. You can stop whenever you want to." He nodded and drank some water. Then he looked the members of the character committee directly in the eyes.

"If I, Kitty's husband, have full confidence in Bill and don't hold him responsible in any way for her death, who are you people to say any different?"

Laura extended her hand to Tommy and

thanked him for his testimony. After he left, she began summing up the evidence. "You have heard ample testimony about the fragile state of Kitty Horton's health. Her husband has just told you about her unstable, high-strung personality. There are literally hundreds of situations that could have triggered the fatal heart attack. If Bill had simply stood there while the woman ranted in the middle of a busy corridor, within earshot of the sick and dying patients and their relatives, blocking the aisle, and impeding the flow of vital traffic, what would have happened next?"

She looked around the room, inviting her listeners to figure it out for themselves. Then she nodded. "That's right. The nurse would have called the guards. They might have grabbed her by the shoulders. They might have triggered the fatal attack. Please think about that for a moment. Instead of suffering the imprisonment of one of your finest doctors, with a flawless medical record, you might have had to contend with something entirely different."

She paused as the doctors absorbed what she had been saying and began to nod to each other. "You would have been slapped with a lawsuit. A smart attorney could have accused you of hiring guards who manhandle visitors."

At the end of Laura's summation, she excused herself so as to allow the board to discuss matters among themselves for the next few days. This would give them time to call new witnesses or recall old ones, to shed additional light on the matter at hand.

Mickey wanted to review with her everything that had been said. First, though, he insisted on taking her out for dinner. "You must be completely wiped out, darling," he said. "Let me fill you up with some good food so that you can fill me in on how you handled the character board."

Laura gave him the highlights. Even from the little she told him, she could see how impressed he was. "You know, dear," he said when she was finished talking, "I sure am pleased that you never decided to take up the law as a profession. You could have run me out of court. You are just too good for words!"

Evidently the board agreed: Bill had paid his debt to society for an accidental gesture which had had nothing to do with his medical work. They reinstated his license with two important provisions. First, he was to consider himself on three years' probation. Second, as a condition for allowing him to practice medicine at the hospital, he had to submit to periodic counseling and testing from a qualified psychiatrist.

The board didn't bother looking very far before settling on a qualified psychiatrist. Laura had so intelligently championed Bill's cause, and studied him so thoroughly, it would be up to her to continue that work by overseeing his case and reporting back to them.

Would this never end? Laura wondered. Her cooperation was needed in order for Bill to resume his career. Having agreed to help earlier, she was hard put to find a reason to reject the assignment now. Lately she had begun to dream about Bill, about the years together upstate when they had shared dreams of opening a joint medical practice, and the future had seemed to be theirs for the taking.

The party celebrating the verdict was at Addie's new home. It was small, as Horton family parties went. Tommy begged off—he had promised to take his daughter on a camping trip. "Besides," he confided to Bill when he congratulated him, "I'm not used to crowds yet, even if it's just the family. I like to take people one or two at a time." Bill said he understood, and assured Tommy that there were no hard feelings.

Julie claimed to be still in mourning for Scott. Doug and Addie had their own ideas about that, but they let it go. It might be years before the three of them could sit down together to break bread and share happy feelings. They were in no rush and neither was she.

Alice and Tom were on hand at Addie's to greet Laura and Mickey. Bill had gone out to get flowers for his hostess, and when he returned, he and Laura greeted each other guardedly, with a superficial appearance of warmth, but no kissing. The others were occupied and didn't notice. He was grateful in a way that they hadn't brought the baby. He didn't know how well he could take his first meeting with his secret son.

Everyone admired the formal living room, replete with satin-covered sofas and needlepoint chairs. Then Addie led them to the sun room, a large indoor patio furnished in lemon and light green with brilliantly colored flowers spilling out of hanging wicker baskets.

A baby grand piano stood in one corner, on it the music for all the old favorites that Addie and Doug loved so much. When Addie was sure that Doug had had a drink or two and felt mellow and relaxed, she made her way over to the piano. "Come on, honey, let's perform," she said with a smile. When he hesitated, she urged, "It's just for the family. We enjoy it so much when we're alone. Let's spread the happiness. Don't begrudge those nearest and dearest to me."

Doug shrugged and made his way over to the piano. Addie struck a few familiar chords by way of an introduction, smiling up at him. His sweet, lilting voice leaned into the music and soon the room was filled with song. Mickey extended his hand to Laura, and they began dancing. Tom Horton reached for Alice, and they became the second couple on the floor. Addie, seeing Bill standing alone, called him over. "Come on, you read music well enough to turn the pages for me."

One after another, Doug sang all the Frank Sinatra and Mel Tormé favorites, with some old Rodgers and Hammerstein thrown in for good measure. And before long, he was too enmeshed in the magic to retain any self-consciousness. He relaxed and began gesturing, underlining the tender phrases and giving emphasis where it was needed.

"Hey, you're terrific!" Mickey yelled across the room as he led Laura through a series of intricate dips and swirls.

"Not bad, old buddy," Bill twinkled in a low voice. "I never would have thought you had it in you."

Alice and Tom stopped for a moment, breathless after a long, fast number. They stood in the center of the room and applauded.

Mickey said, "Hey, I just wish the old Lime-light Cafe were still open. We could take Doug down there and show them a thing or two about how a song should really sound."

"I remember the Limelight. I used to go there as often as I could get someone to take me," Addie said. "When did it close?"

"Old Man Knowlton would know," Doug piped up. "I don't know anything about the place, but it's listed with us. The owners retired to Florida a few months ago."

Laura walked over to Doug and shook his hand. "You're truly marvelous," she said. "You're easily as good as any professional singer."

Addie was the first to agree. More than that, she showed how much she meant it. The next day she stopped in at Knowlton's and bought Doug his own nightclub—she had finally found him a career.